Magpie's Blanket

Magpie's Blanket

A NOVEL

Kimberly D. Schmidt
with Jennifer A. Whiteman
Foreword by Henrietta Mann

University of New Mexico Press • Albuquerque

Library of Congress Cataloging-in-Publication Data
Schmidt, Kimberly D., 1961–
Magpie's blanket : a novel / Kimberly D. Schmidt ; with Jennifer A. Whiteman ; foreword by
Henrietta Mann.
pages cm
Includes bibliographical references and index.
ISBN 978-0-8263-5632-1 (pbk. : alk. paper) — ISBN 978-0-8263-5633-8 (electronic)
1. Cheyenne Indians—Fiction. I. Whiteman, Jennifer A. II. Title.
PS3619.C4457M34 2016
813'.6—dc23
2015017188

Cover illustration: *Sioux squaws killed*, ledger art from the book
*People of the Sacred Mountain: A History of the Northern Cheyenne Chiefs
and Warrior Societies, 1830–1879* by Father Peter John Powell.
Book design by Catherine Leonardo
Composed in Minion Pro 10.5/14
Display type is Present LT Std

For Peace Chief Lawrence Hart, the inspiration for "Two Feathers," Dr. Henrietta Mann, distinguished Cheyenne activist and educator, and for all those who survived and told the story.

Proceeds from the author's royalties will be donated to benefit the Cheyenne Cultural Center in Clinton, Oklahoma.

Foreword

—

Magpie's Blanket is a story about the harrowing survival of a young Cheyenne woman, as well as the power of healing. Her fictional story is couched within the appalling historical facts of the massacre of a peaceful band of Cheyenne led by Mo'ohtavetoo'o, Black Kettle, a peacekeeper and diplomat of the highest order.

This is also a personal story because I am a direct descendant of a survivor Homa'oestaa'e, called White Buffalo Woman. She was my great-grandmother, the grandmother of my father, Mo'ehno'hamemeo'o, Horse Road, and the mother of his father, Vovo'hase'hame'e, Spotted Horse. Another survivor was my other great-grandmother, Vister, the grandmother of my mother, Day Woman, whose father was Deer. For me, any day is a good time to remember the past, to be thankful for today, and to create understanding for a better tomorrow.

There are many accounts of the massacres and atrocities committed against the Cheyenne at Sand Creek and at the Washita. These accounts are generally written by men and focus on failed treaties, military campaigns and skirmishes, and the men who waged them. Yet none tell the story from a young woman's or child's perspective, though it was primarily these individuals who were affected most by the attacks.

My great-grandmothers never forgot the horror of the slaughter of these murderous assaults. Cheyenne people remember and will always remember the Washita Massacre, just as they will never forget the massacre at Sand Creek. Those two events are real to us and are a part of our blood, just as they are close in memory. No one can change what happened at those places. History cannot be changed. However, we can learn lessons in promoting positive international treaty relations and interpersonal relations.

These two brave-hearted Cheyenne women lived in a tumultuous time fraught with peacekeeping intentions, which somehow resulted in an ever-shrinking land base. We think White Buffalo Woman was born in what was then Wyoming Territory. Her headstone in the Hammon Indian Mennonite Cemetery states she was born in 1853. She was a respected midwife who "caught many a baby" in her strong hands with long fingers. Much like the country doctor of the times, she made house calls in a wagon and horses driven by her son. She also had good horse medicine and was a recognized healer of horses, which were significant to "horse culture" people.

It is said White Buffalo Woman was born two years after the great Horse Creek Treaty to a Cheyenne father, Eagle Mann, and part-Sioux mother by the name of Red Bead. The family belonged to the Wotapio band, which the older people called the Cheyenne-Sioux Band. The band name was actually a Sioux word that meant "eaters," or some say "those who eat with the Sioux." The Wotapio were known for their exceptional tipis, equally first-rate possessions, and fine horse herds.

They moved with the buffalo on lands guaranteed by the Horse Creek Treaty, which straddled parts of Wyoming, Nebraska, Colorado, and Kansas. A flood of emigrants was flowing across their hunting territories. The Cheyenne called them *ve'ho'e*, which ironically is the same word for spider.

In the meantime Black Kettle, a So'taa'e man and member of the Elk Horn Scrapers warrior society, married Medicine Woman Later, a woman from the Wotapio band. As was customary, he joined her people. Following the death of Bear Feather in 1854, Black Kettle became his successor as chief of the Wotapio band, thus becoming a member of the Council of Forty-Four chiefs, established by the Cheyenne prophet Motse'eoeve, Sweet Medicine.

Vister was a contemporary of White Buffalo Woman, and they were born at a challenging time in tribal history. Vister was a teenager when the massacre at Sand Creek took place. My mother would recount her story, and she said when Vister recalled the Sand Creek attack she would talk of the immense sense of security and safety she felt as they settled in that night before the onslaught. However, the dawn brought terror when they were surprised by the vicious attack by Colonel Chivington, in which he ordered his men to take no prisoners.

Vister told of her uncle coming to her with a pony and placing her on it; he told her to flee and smacked the hindquarters of the horse. Instead, she looked for her younger brother. She located him and dashed toward him, and pulled him up behind her as bullets were flying all around them. As they raced away, one bullet found its mark and lodged in her calf.

As the children fled from the surrounded camp, Black Kettle congregated some members of his band around his lodge, from which a large American flag and a smaller white flag fluttered from a tall lodgepole; nevertheless, the bloodbath continued unabated, with no sign of mercy or compassion. When the firing ceased, more than 137 lay dead, of whom only twenty-eight were men; the remainder was helpless women and children.

Vister and her brother escaped on horseback, yet my great-grandmother White Buffalo Woman most likely survived by running with her family to the sandy banks above the river, and along with others digging, with her bare hands, a makeshift bunker. A few of the Cheyenne men had weapons and defended the women and children in this bunker. A member of Black Kettle's band, White Buffalo Woman was but a child of eleven on that fateful morning of November 29, 1864. After Sand Creek, until the day she died, she always slept with her moccasins on.

John Smith, an interpreter, described the atrocities in his testimony before a US congressional committee: "All manner of depredations were inflicted on their persons; they were scalped, their brains knocked out; the men used their knives, ripped open women, clubbed little children, knocked them in the head with their guns, beat their brains out, mutilated their bodies in every sense of the word." To escape this violence, Black Kettle fled south from Sand Creek in Colorado to what is now Oklahoma. Black Kettle's peaceful efforts proved futile.

Four years later, White Buffalo Woman's village was again brutally massacred, this time on the banks of the Washita River. As she had previously, White Buffalo Woman ran and once again she survived. Just as they had at Sand Creek, some of her tribe perished on the banks of the river, including Black Kettle and his wife.

One hundred years later, during a reenactment of the Washita Massacre, an impromptu reconciliation took place. This rarely reported reconciliation resulted in the repatriation of a Washita Massacre victim's bones and helped lay to rest animosities between the Southern Cheyenne and the

Grandsons of the Seventh Cavalry—the descendants of those who had killed Black Kettle and his people. Gifts were exchanged. In Cheyenne tradition, a blanket was given.

As Cheyenne people, we can rejoice over the fact that the Cheyenne way of life was not extinguished in 1864, 1868, or since *ve'ho'e* contact. We continue to maintain our annual traditional ceremonies, and the Council of Forty-Four still functions as the traditional government. Reconciliation and the concepts of restorative justice and peacemaking are key components of the Cheyenne cultural belief system. We remember the teachings of Sweet Medicine, and even though the bison have disappeared as he said they would, we are resilient, we adapt and carry on.

Henrietta Mann, PhD
President, Cheyenne & Arapaho Tribal College
Weatherford, Oklahoma

Introduction

A peace chief stands on a knoll overlooking a gentle river. The waters stream around the base of low hills covered with early grass, and through large stands of cottonwood trees greening with growth. The wind blows fiercely as it often does in Oklahoma.

The peace chief turns and sings to the four sacred directions. His words lift high into the air and then, floating back down, settle into his heart. He pauses. Then he speaks. His voice is quiet, but it carries power, and the small gathering of people leaning against the wind listen intently. Each recognizes the eloquence of the storyteller, the significance of the story.

This is not our story to tell. It belongs to the Southern Cheyenne and the Grandsons of the Seventh Cavalry, those whose ancestors were involved in the historical events depicted in these pages.

This is our story to tell. Unlike so many stories about the Plains Indians and the white invasion, this story ends not only in bloodshed and violence. Ultimately, it ends in a difficult and lasting healing ceremony. This story speaks of a deliberate creation of peace between two people who had long been enemies.

This story has circled through the generations. It is a story retold from oral accounts passed from grandparents to children. As with all stories for the ages, each generation must discover for themselves the narrative's power and relevance.

This story is for all of us to tell and tell it we should.

PART ONE

1868 and 1864

Chapter One

Washita, 1868

THE SKY SWALLOWED the sun, wrapping the yellow orb's brilliance in moody, slate-colored tones, pressing it down close to the earth and preventing it from arching high into the sky. Gradually the sun tired, faded, and the sky and earth became one color—the color of snow, the color of storms on the horizon. Magpie shivered in the icy cold as she petted the muzzle of her small cream-colored pony that was standing quietly near her tipi. "You're looking a little thin. Were you warm last night? How's the winter grass? We're both foragers now, aren't we?" Her pony nickered and shook her mane, as if responding to Magpie's questions.

A group of young men had gathered across the circle from Magpie's tipi. Big Hawk stood in the center of the group. A head taller than most of his companions, he was easy to spot. Magpie found herself watching him. He stood close to the others and they spoke in low tones. Some carried guns; others had bows strung across their backs. Behind them their fastest ponies stood untethered, saddled and ready. Magpie couldn't hear them but she knew they were planning a hunt. She saw a few gestures and nods of approval. A decision had been made and the hunters quickly and silently left the circle. As Big Hawk mounted his pony, he saw Magpie. He raised his free hand in a friendly acknowledgment. Their eyes met and his glance shifted from friendship to something deeper and questioning. Suddenly self-conscious, Magpie lowered her gaze. When she looked up again all she saw was his long straight back as he led his companions, all on horseback, away from the camp. Magpie shook her head and muttered to her pony in frustration. "If he's interested in courting me, why doesn't he speak up? He doesn't speak. He just looks."

Magpie's little sister, Cricket, poked her head through the door flap and grinned. "Does your pony speak Cheyenne or are you talking to yourself again?" she teased. Magpie smiled at her sister. "Always. It helps me think. Come on. Let's go to the river. Our *nahaa'e* needs wood." In response to Magpie's voice, the pony twitched her ears in agreement and shook her mane as if to say, *Yes, I'm ready. Let's go.* Cricket laughed at the pony. "You're lucky your pony talks to you and the cold air doesn't bother her. Can I ride her, please?"

"Sure. We'll all go together. Toss out that dead water from our *nahaa'e*'s kettle. We'll get fresh living water for the day."

Cricket fetched the gleaming kettle and jumped bareback onto the pony, as graceful as a leaf floating onto a lazy stream. Magpie admired her little sister's movements. Where Magpie was quick and decisive, Cricket was elegant and always took her time. Magpie often wished she had her little sister's grace.

The pony, well trained and sensing adventure, waited attentively for Magpie's direction. Her winter coat was rough and long and the breath from her nostrils hung in the cold air before fading away in soft wisps. Magpie thought about the cozy nest she had made during the night, deep within her buffalo robes, next to her sister. It had not been easy uncurling from those thick robes and crawling out into weather so frigid even the hard-packed bare earth inside the tipi crunched under her feet.

An empty cooking pot over dead coals had provoked Magpie out of the tipi and into the gray dawn. Her band needed firewood. Magpie's band was made up of a small group of families. Together they followed the game trails during the summer and camped near rivers during the winter. Troubles with whites—the *ve'ho'e,* or Spider People—meant that hunters and warriors were few, almost as scarce on the plains as the game the men in Magpie's band sought. Many of the older men had gone with Big Hawk's uncle, Black Kettle, to talk to the *ve'ho'e* army men.

Magpie turned her pony toward her favorite foraging grounds, the grove of trees near the Washita River. The pony snorted and trotted through the snow. She knew where she was going. As Magpie led the pony with Cricket astride she found herself thinking once again about Big Hawk. He was of the same band, though not related. They were almost as close as kin. Now that he was a young man, it seemed Big Hawk no longer had time for her. Big Hawk was earning a reputation as a good hunter. Magpie anticipated that one day he would drop off meat, perhaps a buffalo head, by a young woman's tipi, signaling that he was skilled enough to support a family and indicating his intention to marry. Magpie found herself thinking about him more than she wanted to. That look—what did it mean? Even though he was not related and could court her should he choose to, he was too close to her family. He was almost like a brother. She deliberately turned her thoughts to Black Kettle.

Black Kettle was like a grandfather to her. Magpie thought about how brave Black Kettle was and how honorable. Against the wishes of many Cheyennes, Black Kettle had signed treaties promising not to make trouble with the *ve'ho'e*. *On how many treaties had he made his mark?* Magpie wondered. "Perhaps now those Spider People will leave us alone. Perhaps now it will be safe to sleep without my moccasins on," muttered Magpie to herself. At the sound of Magpie's voice Cricket smiled and the pony snorted and twitched her ears.

Magpie led the pony down the slow rises of the Horseshoe Hills to the Washita River. The hills reminded Magpie of her camp's traditional winter encampment along the Antelope Hills. The Antelope Hills were named for the graceful and quickly darting animals Magpie remembered as having been abundant when her band first came to the Washita to camp. Then, the animals had run freely on these hills and in great numbers. Once when walking on the hills, Magpie had stumbled upon two baby antelope, twins nestled side by side, not making a move in the protective grass cover. She had quickly apologized and excused herself, not wanting to harm the little ones. Now, just a few years later, the only things found on the Antelope Hills were bones. Dry, white bones. *Ve'ho'e* fur traders, who took only hides, and hunters, those who killed for pleasure, left the animals on the plains to rot. *I wonder what I'll find on these hills today*, Magpie thought.

As she walked in front of the pony, the sun made one last stand, peeking out from behind heavy, dense clouds and ever so briefly transforming the softly sculpted, snow-covered gray hills to crystalline white. Magpie squinted against the shining snow. Then she slowed to a standstill, not quite believing her eyes. "Look." She dropped the reins and pointed. There over the next ridge, on the opposite side of the river, was a trail. From where Magpie stood it looked like a path deeply rutted in the snow, possibly a trail made by wagons and horses. Were *ve'ho'e* around? What were they doing here? This could only mean one thing. If *ve'ho'e* were here, Magpie's band would need to move closer to the other tribes. Alone along the Washita River the small band of families to which Magpie belonged were unprotected and vulnerable to attack. Magpie shivered again, this time from fear.

Now that she had spotted the trail, she walked faster and with determination. She grabbed the pony's reins and, urging the animal along, plowed through the snow, her legs churning. Cricket rode mutely. She did not need Magpie to explain her motives. Both girls knew they would have to quickly gather wood and water and make it back to the protection of the camp. On this dull wintry day, as Magpie strode toward the tracks she remembered her name and drew strength from her naming story.

Minutes after Magpie was born a bird walked boldly into her mother's isolated birthing hut on the edges of the camp. Magpie's mother giggled. Sage Woman was usually quiet and reticent, the kind of woman who fades into the background. But the bird's antics were a relief after hours of labor and Sage Woman welcomed the unusual feathered visitor. At Sage Woman's laughter Medicine Woman Later looked at her in surprise then straightened from her work where she had been tending a cooking pot over the fire.

At first Medicine Woman Later tried to gently encourage the bird out of the hut. "Shoo, shoo, Brother Magpie," Medicine Woman Later gently coaxed. "There's nothing for you here." The bird seemed reluctant and kept looking at the new baby lying on Sage Woman's slack belly. Finally, Medicine Woman Later, usually a patient woman, said pointedly, "Go away. What do you know about little babies?" She grabbed a blanket she had brought with her and swiped at the bird. The bird hopped forward. He seemed bold and unconvinced by Medicine Woman Later's scolding. He pecked at a basketful of brightly colored beads that had been placed near Sage Woman's feet. Sage Woman grinned at the bird.

"I mean it. Go away." Medicine Woman Later swiped at him once again forcing him out of the hut but not before he had two beads firmly in his beak.

"What a pretty blanket. I like the bold colors." Sage Woman reached for the blanket. She unfolded it and watched its stripes dance in the dim light of the hut. The vivid swathes of yellow and red were bisected by a bold black center stripe. Sage Woman ran her hand over the blanket and smiled. Medicine Woman Later was surprised at Sage Woman's reaction. Sage Woman usually preferred muted colors and earth tones. Perhaps the new baby girl was speaking through her mother.

"You may have it," Medicine Woman Later said. "Keep it as a gift from me for your new daughter. When she is a year old, we'll honor her birth with a giveaway. After that she'll have many blankets. Keep this one as her 'first-year blanket,' something to keep her warm until then.

"Let me see the child." Medicine Woman Later fussed over and cuddled the baby. Then she began washing the infant. She had warmed water in her large copper kettle. She took a soft deerskin cloth and dipped it in the water. Sponging the baby with the wet cloth, she admired the newborn's thick black hair and perfect tiny body. After she bathed the baby Medicine Woman Later massaged the baby's skin with grease made of boiled-down buffalo fat. The grease protected the newborn's skin. When the baby was covered head to toe in grease, Medicine Woman Later powdered the baby with a dusting of the prairie puffball, a mushroom commonly found on hillsides nearby. It had been dried and pounded into the finest flour. Finally, she swaddled the baby in an absorbent rabbit-fur diaper before tightly wrapping her, head to toe, in the colorful blanket. Then she gently placed the baby snuggly into a decorated cradleboard. Medicine Woman Later brought the infant to her mother, smiling in anticipation of being the young one's nahaa'e, of helping her closest friend raise the girl-child in traditional Cheyenne ways.

"She is a healthy girl. Her umbilical cord will soon fall off. Have you finished beading her medicine pouch?" Medicine Woman Later asked Sage Woman.

Sage Woman smiled. "It is almost ready. That crazy bird stole some of the beads I wanted for it." Sage Woman was proud of her new daughter but was reluctant to show it. She paused then noted, "She is such a good baby. She has yet to cry,"

"She is a true Cheyenne baby," agreed Medicine Woman Later, glancing up from her work. "She does not whimper and we will never need to leave her in the bushes away from the camp until she learns to stop crying."

The next day the magpie came back. The sun's rays warmed the ground in a reverse weave pattern of the hut's loosely constructed reed walls. Once again the bird hopped boldly inside, ruffling his black and brilliant blue wing feathers, his long dark iridescent tail bobbing up and down. He looked around, his sharp eyes seeming to take in everything in the dim light, like a ve'ho'e trader fingering buffalo robes for sale. What might he steal and fly away with today? Perhaps some porcupine quills? "Shoo, you crazy bird." Medicine Woman Later picked up the blanket again. "You think you are the midwife? I am the midwife. You are a great helper but I know about babies. When you help birth babies, then you can come and visit. And when you come, make sure you bring an honor gift for the little one." Medicine Woman Later scolded him, "No more stealing either." The bird cocked his head at Medicine Woman Later and considered her speech. Then he hopped even closer to the baby, craning his head back and forth and looking inquisitively at her before nabbing a crumb of skillet bread in his beak and flying away. Sage Woman erupted in laughter at Medicine Woman Later. "He doesn't listen to you," she practically cawed at her friend. As Chief Black Kettle's wife and a highly respected woman in her own right, Medicine Woman Later was used to having a voice in the camp and getting her way.

"Brother Magpie is like a Cheyenne Dog Soldier. He does what he wants," the new mother observed.

The next day the bird came back again, but this time he was not alone. He brought his mate. The two birds cavorted in the hut, fanning their brilliant tail feathers, cooing and chortling. Sage Woman was ready to welcome the birds. She had put a few kernels of corn out for them. As she lay on layers of buffalo robes with the baby snuggled against the small of her back, the birds hopped nearer. She sat up and told the birds, "I know you keep visiting to make sure our little daughter will be well loved. Believe me, I will be a very good mother to your little Magpie. See, her eyes are dark and fierce, just like yours. She is intelligent and quick. She will be a helper to the Tsitsistas—the People—just like you are, Magpie Bird. The People are grateful for your help. Because of you, the Tsitsistas eat meat and not grass. I am a quiet woman, but I will raise her to be bold, just like you. I will ask Medicine Woman Later to whisper a name in her ear during her naming ceremony. For you she will be named." The birds cocked their heads. It seemed they were listening to Magpie's mother, as if they understood her

words. Then bobbing the corn down into their gullets, they flew away. The
next day they did not come back and Sage Woman knew she had made
peace with the birds.

Over the years, Magpie grew into her name. She often visited the birds'
winter nesting site in the hackberry shrub trees and high in the cottonwoods along the creek beds. There she sat and watched patiently. She
watched them gather for winters of visiting, just like her people. When the
magpies were agitated, she thought of them as dancing and singing their
old songs, flapping their wings and hopping from branch to branch.
Magpie liked to mimic their sounds and motions and often entertained her
family with her imitations. Sometimes Magpie thought, with all their yak-
king and screeching, they even told stories, just like her elders, only a lot
louder. The bird, Cheyennes knew, was intelligent, curious, and fearless.
When the pony reached the top of the ridge Magpie turned to look back to
where she had started. In this part of the country the hills rolled evenly,
small and gentle against the gray sky. Magpie again was struck at how the
sky and earth were the same color, blending together as one. Finding the
horizon was difficult.

"The same color, a warning for more snow, for heavy storms," said
Magpie. She knelt down in the snow and studied the tracks. There were
wagon wheels, horseshoes, and army boots. The sight transported her back
to another river, another open prairie, and another wintry day when the
earth and sky were one. As she studied the tracks, she shuddered. She
looked into her sister's eyes and saw her own fear reflected in her sister's
dark eyes. Then she reassured herself, *I need to be bold. I need to be a magpie. I am a magpie. I am Magpie.*

Chapter Two

～

Sand Creek, 1864

MAGPIE REMEMBERED THE sun had been setting low along Sand Creek. Below the clouds, the sun cast clear and deep colors onto the tipis and across the grasses. During the evening hours she liked to walk to the embankments of the creek, situated high above the camp. There she would sit and watch as the band's tipis, lit from fires within, began to glow like pale lanterns against a darkening night sky. Only after the sun had completely set would she return to camp.

Cheyenne women were proud of their tipi-making skills. The bleached, brilliantly white hides stretched taut over large lodgepole pine trunks made from the trees named for their principal use in daily life. Some of the lodgepoles had been in the band for generations. Carefully cured and carved, they were handed down from mother to daughter. The poles were thick and heavy. Many of them had been harvested from the mountains to the north and west of the band's roaming lands. It took a number of men several weeks to travel to the pine groves, identify the best trees, cut them down, and drag them home behind the sturdy pack ponies. Some of the tipis were decorated, and others were stark white, but each one reflected their maker's pride in craftsmanship.

Magpie could always spot her tipi. White Antelope, her father, was an artist and liked to paint. Sage Woman's bleached-white tipi was one of the most decorated in the camp. Magpie had many memories of him carefully decorating her mother's tipi where the family lived. First, he traced the figures on the tipi with charcoal. Then, carefully dipping his handmade brushes into paint, he filled in the figures with color. His victories in battle and on the hunt circled the sides of her mother's tipi. It embarrassed Sage Woman to live in such a colorful home, but White Antelope insisted. Sage Woman was proud of his artistry even though she was uncomfortable with her husband's need for display. White Antelope had asked Medicine Woman Later to add sacred symbols to his artwork. Whenever Sage Woman lit the fire, buffalo, medicine wheels, animals, arrows, and stars seemed to dance across the stretched canvas in response to the flickering flames. Walls of woven reeds and rushes acted as windbreaks in the winter and surrounded the tipis on their north and west sides. Even these windbreaks were carefully constructed and decorated. Ornamental talismans, small calico bundles filled with tobacco, were hung to protect the inhabitants of the tipi.

That evening on the northern plains it was cold. Magpie had decided not to trudge up the hill to watch the sun set over dancing stars and circling medicine wheels. Magpie remembered she had been a child, carefree and at play, in spite of the cold.

Magpie shifted her stance and placed her little sister on the ground. "Run, Cricket, run and hide." She helped her little sister learn the game. "You have to run as fast as you can and find a good hiding place." Cricket ran a few paces. "I hid. I here. Come and find me." Cricket had placed her blanket on the ground in the middle of the camp. Her body formed a small lump under the blanket she dragged everywhere with her. One of the camp dogs started to sniff at the blanket. Magpie ran to Cricket and scooped her up in her arms and tickled her.

"Cricket, you need to find a place to hide. A better place. A place that is not in the way of everything and everybody." Magpie laughed as she spoke. "Big Hawk and the other young men will stumble over you when they come home from their hunt. If they bring home big game, they'll be so happy they won't notice you. If you stay here, the old women who can't see or walk so good will trip over you." Cricket nodded solemnly, her eyes big and round. Magpie continued her instruction. "When you find that place be quiet. Not a sound. Don't let anyone know you are there." Placing her sister back on the ground she said seriously, "This game is important, Cricket."

Cricket toddled off, dragging her blanket behind her. Magpie watched her sister, noting her little legs and rounded body. Cricket's gait was that of the very young—more of a waddle than a walk. Cricket dropped to the ground and slid under a wagon, then placed her blanket carefully near a wheel and crawled beside it. Magpie grinned. *Now we are getting somewhere*, she thought. *The child is catching on*. No sooner had the thought entered her head when Cricket called out as loud as she could.

"Here I am, Magpie. Come find me. I hid." Magpie smiled and, shaking her head, ran to Cricket. Once she reached Cricket she cuddled the child in her arms and whispered. "Oh, what a wonderful hiding place, Cricket, but don't tell anyone where you are. In this game we don't let anybody know where we are. We stay hidden. We stay quiet. Try again."

"Okay, Magpie," Cricket whispered back. She was quiet for just a bit. She shifted under her blanket and then she called out, "I hid now. Come and find me."

"I've got you. I've got you, got you, got you!" Magpie laughed as she tussled and tickled her little sister. "You are such a funny little girl. Try one more time. This time, go hide, but don't tell me where you are! You must not tell me where you are hidden. This is important, Cricket. This is a game all Cheyenne children must learn. Listen, Cricket, you must learn this, do you hear?"

Medicine Woman Later, who had been working around her tipi, straightened up and observed, "Our little Cricket always needs to chirp. Magpie, you are more like your mother, you observe and listen. You learned as a small child how to speak with your eyes. We don't need to talk much, do we?"

Magpie smiled with recognition. She was more like her mother, content to watch, ponder, and hold her thoughts. Or, perhaps it was because she was older and trained to keep her thoughts to herself. She looked around the camp and saw Cricket's little lump under her blanket, back in the middle of the camp, the curious dog once again sniffing at the little girl's still form.

Magpie started toward her but her path was blocked by a large, dark muscular form. Big Hawk ran toward the middle of the camp, intercepted Magpie, and scooped up Cricket, blanket and all, onto his shoulders. As he ran he turned toward Magpie and, half shouting, half laughing, said, "Here you go, Cricket. You sit on my shoulders, and we'll teach that crazy Magpie a lesson. Better run, Magpie, because this hawk has nabbed a cricket. Now it's the magpie's turn." Magpie's dark eyes widened. What was Big Hawk doing here? Why wasn't he on the hunt with the others? He was nearly a man and should be off with the other older boys today. Wasn't he too old for these games? She quickly dismissed her questions. Even with Cricket riding on his shoulders, Big Hawk was fast. Magpie sprinted away. She darted between tipis and wagons, causing the dogs to sit up and start barking. As quick as a prairie hare Magpie skimmed over the icy ground.

Pockets of snow and the setting sun had created shadows around her mother's tipi. One drift seemed a perfect hiding place. She slid into the shadow and pinned her small, lithe body against the lodgepole. Covered in part by the lingering snow, she blended in with the shadow until she could barely be seen.

As clever as Magpie was, she wasn't clever enough. "Nice try," Big Hawk yelled as he ran toward the tipi. "We've got her now, Cricket." Cricket shrieked with glee and cupped her little hands around Big Hawk's chin. She had a good seat and managed to stay upright as Big Hawk ran. Magpie watched Big Hawk run toward her hiding place, easily tracking her criss-crossing moccasin footprints, so light and small they made no dent in the grass-covered ground. Big Hawk came straight toward her, his long black braids streaming behind him as he ran. Big Hawk was fast, but he was also heavier, and Cricket, though small, added weight. As he ran, he fought the grass in large, ponderous steps, grunting with the effort. This time, in spite of being discovered, Magpie got away. Lighter than Big Hawk and not quite full-grown, she sped across the ground, once again darting in and out between the tipis and the tall walls of protective rushes and reeds. Magpie was not worried about windbreaks and snowstorms. She was worried about getting caught.

Children of all ages joined in the fun. Soon an entire gang of kids risked getting caught by their tall, strong cousin. Magpie raced for the tall wooden pole set in the middle of the camp. Two waving flags, a US flag topping a white flag, the symbol of a peace treaty made with the *ve'ho'e*, were strung to the pole. A few years earlier Big Hawk's uncle, Black Kettle, had signed a treaty, promising that his warriors would not make war on the *ve'ho'e*. "This flag is a sign of peace. White men will know that we mean them no harm. When they see this flag they will know that we want peace and they will not attack us," Black Kettle had declared as he tied the flag to the top of a sturdy lodgepole pine.

The children of the camp absorbed the lesson and used the lodgepole as a safety zone. There they were safe during their games; no one could touch them. Now the white peace flag protected Magpie from Big Hawk. With one hand on the lodgepole, Magpie taunted Big Hawk, "Yeah . . . nice try. You may be bigger but I'm faster. Magpies fly faster than hawks; they're smarter too!"

Instead of responding, Big Hawk stopped and looked at her. He admired her grace, confidence, and slender form, just starting to show womanhood. He somersaulted Cricket off his shoulders. "Here you go, little one. Go back to Magpie while I chase down a few young warriors."

In spite of his words he stepped back a couple of paces and then stood looking at Magpie. Magpie took Cricket's hand and fell silent under his gaze. Confusion and shyness took over. Instead of looking him in the eye she cast her eyes down and away, not knowing how to respond to this young man whom she had known all her life. Then she straightened and looked Big Hawk right in the eye. As she looked at Big Hawk she thought, *I am Magpie, the daughter of White Antelope and Sage Woman. I am capable, self-reliant, and skilled. If Big Hawk wants to court me, he will have to prove himself a worthy suitor.* Big Hawk noticed her change in stature and caught the fierce, defiant look she shot his way. He raised an eyebrow. Without saying a word he knew he had been put on notice, and he smiled. He knew Magpie would not be easily won. She was Cheyenne after all, taught to value her skills, her womanhood, and to honor herself.

Medicine Woman Later sounded an end to the game. "What do I have here?" She laughed at the circling children. "Such snorting and stomping that I think the children are Buffalo People on stampede." Magpie, grateful for Medicine Woman Later's interruption of the looks passing between herself and Big Hawk, led Cricket to Medicine Woman Later's side, who stood in front of her lodge. Medicine Woman Later eyed her nephew. Even though he had chased down half a dozen youngsters, he was not out of breath. She addressed the panting children: "We are fortunate. Big Hawk and the young men brought back deer. We will have stew today." At those words, Big Hawk looked at Magpie in triumph. He tried, unsuccessfully, to hide how proud he was. He was in the age of promise, the age when a young male grows fully into manhood and finds his place in the tribe. Big Hawk had been trained for the hunt since he was seven years old. Providing meat for cooking pots was a sign of manhood. His aunt had referred to him as a man in public, even though it was only in front of children. Soon he would go on a raid, perhaps participate in the Sun Dance, and after that, should he prove himself worthy, join one of the men's societies.

Medicine Woman Later noticed the look on her nephew's face and glanced at Magpie. Medicine Woman Later's eyes were full of inquiry. Not much escaped her attention. She was growing into old age, full of wisdom and wrinkles but also filled with energy and spirit. It was said that Medicine Woman Later, trained in the healing arts, could sense things long before others could. When she talked, the People listened. To Magpie's young eyes, Medicine Woman Later's skin seemed ready to leave her bones. Yet Magpie also noticed she was one of the tallest women in the camp. Tall even for a Cheyenne, Medicine Woman Later was not bent over and stooped with age as many elderly women. When she walked she reminded Magpie of the cottonwood trees that grew into the riverbank at Sand Creek. The trees grew thicker with age, showing their lives in gnarled layers of growth rings. But as they grew, they gained strength. It was these old ones that most ably withstood the fierce winds that blew across the plains, their roots sunk deep into the earth.

Now Magpie was reminded that Medicine Woman Later's eyes missed nothing. Magpie shrugged. Big Hawk had not talked with her. How could she know what Big Hawk intended? "You are a man, Big Hawk," Medicine Woman Later gently reminded him. "Do Cheyenne warriors play such games?" Big Hawk nodded obedience to his aunt. He remembered the day his *naxane* came to him, many years ago, and replaced his toy bows and arrows with real ones. What followed was a time of testing and confusion. Big Hawk still enjoyed children's games even as he sought the status brought by hunting. "Magpie," Medicine Woman Later turned her attention to the girl, "here." She gestured toward the food. Grateful for something to do, Magpie worked alongside her.

That morning Big Hawk and his group of hunters had tracked deer and brought home two large bucks, enough for many families in the camp. As usual, Medicine Woman Later was the first to prepare the deer for skinning. After Big Hawk dropped the dead animals in front of Medicine Woman Later's lodge, she took a large sharp knife, skinned the deer, and carved two mounds of meat for eating fresh. Medicine Woman Later looked at the knife Magpie was to use. As she had for years, Magpie hefted the knife; its weight and handle felt familiar in her hand. She expertly cut what was left of the meat into thin slices. Then she hung the slices to dry on racks made of branches interlaced with sticks. Some of these dried pieces would be ground into *ame*, which was seasoned with herbs and mixed with wild berries. After hanging the meat, Magpie found Medicine Woman Later in her tipi.

A large, gleaming copper cooking pot sat on top of two slow-burning logs. Light-colored small flames danced around the pot. Medicine Woman Later took her ladle in hand and stirred, singing over the meat and blessing the food with her sounds. She added herbs, dried berries, and water to the meat. As she tended the fire, she took care to keep her dress and shawl out of the flames but also stayed near enough to enjoy the warmth of the small cook fire on a day of deepening cold. Soon the tipi was warm. The aroma of the stew made Magpie's mouth water. They had not had fresh meat for weeks now, subsisting on *ame* and prairie turnips dug last summer.

When the stew was cooked, Medicine Woman Later called to the band. Gathered around her were the children, exhausted after their game of chase with Big Hawk. The children were the first to eat. Other women, smelling the meat, came and ate. Sage Woman dipped her spoon in the pot, savoring the bits of venison in the rich broth. She nodded her head at Medicine Woman Later, the only acknowledgment Medicine Woman Later needed to know that the soup was tasty, seasoned to perfection.

To show their care for their families, the men ate last. In return, the band acknowledged that the last to eat were the most honored, the men of standing in the band and those who brought home the meat. Magpie noticed them standing, talking quietly and watching the others eat. Now Big Hawk moved from the children's circle to join the men. For the first time, he stood with the men. Still a little uncertain if he should be in the men's circle, Big Hawk chose his place next to White Antelope, Magpie's father. White Antelope silently gestured his approval to Big Hawk and stepped to one side, making room for the young man he had raised as a son. Big Hawk smiled broadly at White Antelope, pleased that he was accepted. White Antelope reassured Big Hawk, "You hunted well today. Your hunting pony is well trained. You had no fear. You belong here in this circle with the men."

Big Hawk, White Antelope, and the other men watched the women and children eat. They did not show their hunger, though after their days of following the game trails, the men were probably the hungriest of all. Magpie thought about the hunters and how hard they worked to provide meat for the campfires.

Big Hawk looked around the men's circle and sighed. His uncle, Black Kettle, was absent. "Where did he go?" Big Hawk asked. White Antelope looked at his younger tribesman, a mixture of consternation and amusement tracing his face. He knew what was coming next. He said, "The headsmen and your uncle sat in council. It was decided that your uncle should once again try to broker peace."

Big Hawk respected his uncle too much to say anything against him but he could feel his throat tighten as he thought about his uncle's work.

Magpie noticed Big Hawk's growing agitation. Bowl in hand, she moved closer to the men's circle. She wanted to listen.

Instead of talking directly about Black Kettle, Big Hawk pronounced, "I don't believe in peace. What good is it?"

"Peace is safety. That's the good. Black Kettle is trying to secure safety for our families, our band. It would be better if warriors in the other bands also tried the path of peace," White Antelope explained.

Big Hawk replied, "The Dog Soldiers don't need peace. They don't want safety. They want war and they can defend themselves. Black Kettle can't control them. And even if he could, some of us, even here in his own band, don't want this peace." Big Hawk warmed up to his speech, now talking louder so that others outside the men's circle could hear him. "The *ve'ho'e* talk out of both sides of their mouths. They say one thing. They do another. My uncle is chasing peace like water rushing down a hill. It flows away from him. It is too fast. He will never catch it." The more Big Hawk talked the louder he got. White Antelope tried to calm him.

"It is true that the *ve'ho'e* don't keep their word. But what choice do we have? They outnumber us. They have many more soldiers and guns."

"But we, the Tsitsistas, are great warriors. The *ve'ho'e* cannot fight. We can turn the Spider People back. We must."

"You are right. They cannot fight. They can't even track. But even if we turn them back our people will still be hungry. The earth has changed. The waters are bitter. The grasses grow shorter and lack color. All the grass is one color now. You remember what grass used to look like when the buffalo were still here. The great buffalo herds have been split by the *ve'ho'e* trails. This is the first fresh meat we've had in many weeks. We must bend to the *ve'ho'e*. . . . Bend so that we remain. If we keep fighting there will be no one left. The sun will set on us and will not rise again. Our time on earth will be over."

Big Hawk implored his *naxane,* "I ask you, how can the People make peace with wolves? The *ve'ho'e* are not spiders. They are wolves. They tear at everything. Why do we lie down in front of them?"

"Big Hawk, I do not just lie down in front of them. It is true that I will not kill for my people. Killing just brings more killing and in the end solves nothing. But I want you to hear this." White Antelope stepped closer to Big Hawk. His soft voice was insistent and everyone could hear him. "I will die for my people. That is not lying down. It is not running. It is dying for a lasting peace, dying so that my children and my children's children will have a chance to live without war. It is an honorable way to bring peace."

Big Hawk looked skeptical. White Antelope sighed, knowing how obstinate Big Hawk could be. Still, he wanted to somehow reach the younger man. "You know that as a peace chief your uncle cannot fight. It is the Cheyenne way. If a man attacks his children, if a man attacks his wife, he must sit in front of his tipi, light his pipe, and smoke. Black Kettle is following the wisdom of our traditions."

Even though Magpie had heard these words before, she also felt the urge to resist her father. How could Black Kettle and her father not defend their families? How could they just sit in front of their tipis and smoke?

Big Hawk responded with agitation. "I don't believe in those traditions either. Those traditions and stories were given to us long before the *ve'ho'e* came to our lands. Those are old stories for a different place and a different time. They are no good now. We need new traditions, new laws, and new ways to live. "

Big Hawk's pronouncements shocked White Antelope, but he spoke as deliberately and as gently as he could. "You are right; we do need a new way to live but this new way must depend on our traditions. You cannot change a tradition overnight. Our teachings are sacred. Remember the Cheyenne way. You must make decisions to last for seven generations. We do not seek quick, easy answers. We seek what will last the longest, what will help our people many generations from now. That is what your uncle is trying to do. He is peace chief. He is following the teachings of the ancient Cheyennes. He desires to bring peace to you, to his family, to our band so that we will fight no more and suffer no longer. Your uncle is a great man. He has demonstrated his thoughtfulness and wisdom over many years. You are a thinker, like him. Perhaps one day you too will be peace chief."

Big Hawk did not answer White Antelope. Instead, he lifted his gaze and let it rest in the direction of a small grove of trees on the prairie, the death arbors. Suspended high in the trees were scores of hastily built platforms each made of a few long branches. Big Hawk could see the decaying bodies, graves of those who had already passed away that winter. Smaller platforms held the remains of children who had not survived the starvation time. Looking at the death arbors, Big Hawk felt deep waves of sadness and anger. They started in his gut and welled up into his throat. He tried to choke them back but his sadness was too strong and could not be stopped. His feelings came out of his body in a half-choked cry of despair and a half snort of derision. He was immediately mortified, knowing that his emotional reaction would be seen as a sign that he was still a child and could not control himself—that he was not yet a man. He also knew that, although unplanned, his reaction would be viewed as deeply insulting to the older man. In spite of their strongly felt differences, Big Hawk respected White Antelope.

Big Hawk's sounds were heard throughout the tipi. The band members instantly hushed, and Magpie could feel a building sense of anticipation. How would White Antelope handle this challenge from the hotheaded young man he had raised as his own?

Big Hawk looked at his tribesman, his eyes seeking forgiveness, though he could not bring himself to speak it. True to his words, and true to his beliefs, White Antelope merely shook his head, his eyes gentle. He smiled, his face forgiving the impertinence, his hand resting on Big Hawk's shoulder. Medicine Woman Later also felt the tension in the hush and knew that whoever broke the silence must do so carefully. She looked up from her stirring and calmly remarked, "War destroys and it divides. Look how it has divided us. Brother from brother, father from son, kinsman from kinsman. There is too much fear, too much conflict right now. We need the peace my husband seeks, not only to protect us from the *ve'ho'e* but to bring the band and our tribe back to a togetherness we knew before the *ve'ho'e* came."

Big Hawk looked around at the small group of family members gathered in Medicine Woman Later's tipi. He looked at the clothing the children wore, their bare feet, and the tired look on the women's faces. Even though his band was eating now, they were starving, slowly dying out. Many in his band had already died of hunger. Many had died of *ve'ho'e* diseases. Other bands had been completely wiped out. War had come to them in the guise of fear, confusion, and anger—not just with the *ve'ho'e* but also with one another. As Big Hawk looked at the pinched faces illuminated by Medicine Woman Later's fire he thought the end times were a mere breath away. Perhaps, he mused, harmony among the Cheyennes and even among this small band was as fleeting as Black Kettle's peace.

Medicine Woman Later spooned stew onto skillet bread. "Today we eat. Tomorrow some of us may fight but better to bring peace. Starting here. Starting with White Antelope and Big Hawk we will eat together and bring peace. We need all minds. White Antelope has the wisdom of the elders and Big Hawk has the energy of youth. No one's talents shall be wasted." Big Hawk remained standing, uncertain what to do. He looked around the room. White Antelope gestured for him to sit.

Finally Big Hawk found his voice. "I am sorry, my *naxane*, I meant no disrespect." White Antelope answered, "Eat. When empty bellies start talking, it usually leads to grumbling." Both men laughed.

Magpie watched White Antelope and Big Hawk eat, smiling now as the soup warmed their bellies and brought comfort to their thoughts. Suddenly, Magpie was jealous of Big Hawk. She liked to hunt and could shoot as well as Big Hawk. Perhaps she would hunt. Some of the women in her tribe hunted with the men. Some of them brought home meat for tipi cooking fires. Perhaps she would be one of those women. She already had her own ponies. Perhaps she could train one for the hunt. She crept around the outer edges of the tipi thinking about hunting. As she walked, she thought about moving quietly through grasses stiffened by cold air. She began to carefully choose her steps, placing one foot in front of the other, quietly and with deliberation, as if she were on a hunt.

Big Hawk noticed her and drew attention to her pretend stalking. "Dreaming about being a great hunter, are you?"

Magpie blushed and straightened, embarrassed to know that Big Hawk was watching her. She retorted: "I could be a hunter. I can, you know, because I am a Cheyenne." Magpie drew herself up. "I can hunt. I can track. I am a good hunter. Someday I'll have a buffalo pony and I'll train him well."

"Humph." Big Hawk sounded skeptical. "Did you hunt today?"

"Not today. Today I tried to teach Cricket how to hide. Someday I will hunt. Lots of Cheyenne women go on the hunt."

White Antelope looked up from his soup and gently chided Big Hawk. "Magpie's eyes are bright and keen. She is fast and can run for miles. She is already good with the ponies, better than many of the boys. She will make a good hunter."

"Yes, but you should not praise the girl," Medicine Woman Later interjected. "She is young. The praise will make her weak." Sage Woman was surprised to hear Medicine Woman Later speak in such strong tones about Magpie, usually a favored child. Sage Woman did not defend her daughter but looked at White Antelope, her eyes imploring him to confront Medicine Woman Later.

"No, not this one. This one will never show weakness." White Antelope looked at both Big Hawk and his mother, and not quite covering a smile and nodding his head, he said approvingly, "She was born with flint in her bones." Magpie pretended not to notice her father's pronouncement. To blush or respond to praise was not the Cheyenne way, yet his words thrilled her.

Big Hawk, chided for the second time, fell silent. The thrill of standing in the men's circle was gone. He felt thoroughly chastened and was too embarrassed to apologize to Magpie.

White Antelope finished his soup, stood, and addressed Medicine Woman Later. "You are a good chief's wife. Your cooking pot is always full. No one leaves your tipi with an empty stomach." And with that, White

Antelope and Sage Woman left Medicine Woman Later's tipi. They walked the few paces toward the river where Sage Woman's tipi stood sheltered in the trees against the winter winds.

Magpie and Cricket followed their parents back to their mother's tipi. Magpie turned and looked back at Medicine Woman Later's tipi. Big Hawk's favorite hunting pony stood patiently nearby. Big Hawk's taunts still rang in Magpie's ears. Why did he have to tease her so much? He should not pay so much attention to her. He was not her brother. He had no say over her. He should follow traditional ways and pretend to ignore her. She entered the tipi, unlaced and took off her moccasins, and helped Cricket out of hers, placing both pairs with the small bundles Sage Woman kept by their buffalo-robe bed.

"Check your bundle before bed," Sage Woman reminded Magpie.

They never moved the bundles. Always in the same spot, the bundles were a constant reminder of the threat under which Magpie's family lived. In her camp each woman and child had their own bundle. If the *ve'ho'e* should ever come, riding through the camp and shooting their guns, the children knew to grab their bundles and run, run as fast as they could and hide. Magpie sorted through her bundle. It was always the same: moccasins, dried meat, a knife, and a small blanket. Magpie prayed that she'd never have to reach for it.

"It's all here," she called over her shoulder in the direction of her mother.

"As you check your bundle, I'll check my weapons," said her father. The men kept their weapons near the tipi flap, also in a special spot. The weapons were never to be moved.

"Father, I thought you said you would not fight the *ve'ho'e*." Magpie responded. Her voice carried the suggestion of a question.

White Antelope answered, "I will try not to fight. When the fighting comes, then we shall see if I can follow the path to peace."

Magpie moved to her place on the women's side of the tipi and crawled into her buffalo robe. Cricket crawled in beside her and together they made a small hollow deep within the softened fur. She felt Cricket's small body, warm against her skin. They cuddled like animals in a cozy burrow, curled up together to ward off the cold of the night.

Just a few miles away, an army of soldiers, some dressed in worn-out boots and miner's caps, others fully outfitted in military garb, moved stealthily toward Magpie's band. Their leader was a ruthless minister hell-bent on killing "heathen Indians." There, in a brutally cold wind, the men waited for a starless night to give way to early day.

Chapter Three

*

Sand Creek, 1864

MAGPIE WOKE EARLY, padded across the lodge floor from her bed near the back of the tipi, and poked her head out the door flap. She shrugged. It was a gloomy, overcast morning. She glanced at Big Hawk's tipi. Black Kettle's horse stood alone. He had come back during the night. Big Hawk's favorite pony, usually tethered nearby with his uncle's horse, was gone. Had Big Hawk gone hunting again? It seemed so. She looked around. The hunters had left early that morning. All their ponies were gone. The camp was still. Birds perched silently in trees, high above the water. Their dark bodies were somber and still in the cold winter air. She barely had time to note the mood of the morning before she heard cries coming from the center of the camp. She heard single gunshots and then earth-rattling rapid-fire rounds of ammunition. Sage Woman bolted up from her bed and called, "Magpie, Cricket. Grab your bundles. Run. Hide. Do not speak. Do not move. I will find you."

White Antelope sprang from the tipi. He could smell the acrid burning of gunshot in flesh. He looked in the direction of where the shots were fired. Mounted on the ridge were four huge guns. They fired mercilessly into the camp. White Antelope could feel the rumble of horses' hooves as they pounded through the camp, the men shooting as they rode. He saw women and children kneeling on the ground in front of marauding men, begging for mercy. Instinct took over and White Antelope ran for his weapons. As he hefted his gun and spear into his hands, he knew they would do little good. Big Hawk was right. The *ve'ho'e* were tricksters, foolish and ignorant. Promises and treaties were as brittle as eggshells and just as easily broken. The *ve'ho'e* would make war on them despite their promises.

He thought about his people and his family. *My people have no chance. These* ve'ho'e *will kill us all. Rather than fight, I will die with my people. Today is as good as any day to die. I will sing my death song. Where should I die? Where should I make a stand for peace? For peace for my people?* Instead of firing his gun, White Antelope ran toward the white flag. There stood Black Kettle. Black Kettle yelled, "Come stand under the *ve'ho'e* flag and the white flag. Here we are safe. Come stand with me." White Antelope was not as confident in the protection of the flags but, loyal to Black Kettle, he ran for the lodgepole. He was determined that, if he should die, his death would powerfully communicate the struggle of his people. He would not kill, but he would die in an attempt to bring peace. Standing and singing in front of the lodgepole next to Black Kettle, the white flag of surrender fluttering in the cold wind, he thrust his spear into the ground. He turned to Black Kettle. "Go, save those you can. The *ve'ho'e* are ruthless. They do not honor their promises. I will stand here as long as I can."

Black Kettle clasped hands with White Antelope in a silent exchange. Black Kettle knew he would never see his friend again. As Black Kettle led those gathered near the lodgepole away from the camp, White Antelope made his last stand. He faced the oncoming rush of men and horses. White Antelope stood and in a loud, clear voice, his arms outstretched as if to try to stop the madness, sang his death song. He had sung this song many times before as a young warrior, tethered to his spear, taking his stand by fighting in one position until another Cheyenne warrior set him free. This was his last statement.

"Only the earth and mountains last forever."

This time he knew he would not be set free and he would not fight. He would sing until he died.

"Only the earth and mountains last forever."

A man with a dirty face dropped off an ill-kempt horse. White Antelope noticed his patched clothing and miner's cap set askew on his head. The miner advanced toward White Antelope. White Antelope watched him come closer. The miner drew a heavy sword from its scabbard.

"I won't kill you quickly. You will die slowly. Fight, you red coward bastard heathen savage, fight."

White Antelope faced the miner square on, tilted his head back, and sang his song to the heavens.

"Only the earth and mountains last forever."

The miner raised his weapon, brandishing it back and forth. With every cut through the air he stepped closer to White Antelope. White Antelope's voice echoed through the camp. With every note White Antelope's voice got louder and stronger.

"Only the earth and mountains last forever."

The miner raised his saber high above his head. As he did, several shots rang out from behind White Antelope. It seemed the entire army had emptied their guns into White Antelope's body. White Antelope was dead before he hit the ground. As he fell, he slumped against the lodgepole, dying under the white flag.

A smoking gun betrayed a rider who shouted derisively, "Your job is to kill. This is war, not some melodrama!" The miner, frustrated at being bested out of his quarry, but not daring to challenge White Antelope's murderer, took out his fury on White Antelope's dead body. He raised his sword and scalped White Antelope. Then he took his knife and butchered White Antelope's body, severing his genitals from his body. "I'll make his balls into a pouch," the miner gloated.

The army moved through the camp, methodically scalping the men, women, and children as they lay dying. Smelly men in ratty uniforms raped women and girls before killing them. One man paraded a woman's genitals on a wooden stick through the camp. Another cut a fetus from a still-living mother's womb. The mother died, her arms reaching for her already dead baby. Children were slaughtered. One man rode through the camp yelling, "Nits make lice. Nits make lice," as he rode his horse over the fleeing young bodies, cutting them down with his saber, like grass before a scythe.

The earth and mountains last forever, as do songs. White Antelope's song was powerful and did not die with him. Above the din, it hung in the cold air, echoing off the tipis, reverberating above the frozen ground. As Black Kettle's band fled during the onslaught, White Antelope's song pulsed through the camp. Then, the song faded in the pounding of hooves, the shouting, and the shooting. White Antelope's song became softer but it did not disappear. His song blended with the grasses and joined the wind, already a cleansing and healing presence to the bodies of the dead Cheyennes. The song settled into the blood pooling around bodies, the blood that refused to soak into the frozen earth.

〜〜〜

The camp was in chaos. Even in her panic, Magpie noticed that the swarms of men on horseback did not all wear the blue clothing and brass buttons of the US Army. They seemed to be undisciplined and disheveled. Magpie could feel the cold wind freezing her cheeks as she lurched forward, her small bundle in one hand, and Cricket's soft hand in the other. She heard Sage Woman's footsteps behind her and exhaled with relief as her mother grabbed Cricket's other hand. Together they ran through the camp, to the very edges of the tipis, heading to the open prairie, away from the trees and the protection of Sand Creek.

A large swayback bay mare galloped up beside them, a drunken man on her back. The mare reared when the man tried to run them over. Sage Woman threw Magpie and Cricket under her body as the man, cursing, emptied his gun into her back and neck. Sage Woman, silent even when dying, did not cry out.

Two small bodies were pinned under their mother. Magpie could barely breathe. She held Cricket close. "Don't say a word. Do not speak, my little Cricket." Sage Woman's body and her colorful blanket protected her daughters, hiding them and keeping them warm. Magpie felt her mother's warmth gradually fade as Sage Woman's blood drained into the snow. When Sage Woman drew her last breath, she whispered the names of White Antelope, Magpie, and Cricket over and over. Then, so quietly that Magpie could barely hear her, she whispered, "Stay still. Stay still like baby antelope hiding on the prairie. Do not move until someone comes back for you. My body will protect you." She closed her eyes and spoke no more.

Magpie was too much in shock to register what had just happened, but somehow she knew her mother was still with her, even in death, watching to make sure she was safe. She murmured over and over, "Play the game, Cricket. Don't move. Don't say a word." Cricket's small body was rigid but gradually she relaxed under her mother's protective blanket, cradled in Magpie's arms.

28

At first the girls could hear the sounds of battle all around. They recognized the cries of their friends being slaughtered and mutilated by the marauding horde. After a short while Magpie could smell the acrid scent of burning leather and she knew they were burning the tipis. After midday, the men finished with their looting and killing and the camp quieted as they rode off. Nothing stirred. All was silent. Even the unceasing wind stilled. Finally, Magpie dared to come out from under her mother's body. When she tried to lift her head she could barely move. Her body tingled from hours of holding still, barely daring to breathe, holding Cricket firmly against her. As she emerged from under the blanket, Magpie saw two figures walking through the camp. Big Hawk had come back with his uncle.

Magpie was surprised to see that Black Kettle wore the medal given to him by the *ve'ho'e* president. *He should burn that for all it's worth*, she thought. *Burn it with everything else that's been burned.* Then she noticed his gait. He moved with deep sorrow and anguish, stooping to check each body, holding his hand under each nose, hoping to feel the slightest breath. He stayed with each body, running his hands over the corpse and praying before moving on to another still form. She overheard Black Kettle tell Big Hawk, "Perhaps a few of our people are not dead but only wounded."

Big Hawk walked around the dead bodies, stunned at what he saw. He noticed Sage Woman's blanket. Its bold stripes stood out against the muted ground. The blanket covered Sage Woman like a shroud. He noticed a small movement and, trained for the hunt, he stopped and watched until he understood what was happening. He saw Sage Woman's form divide into two then three, a lithe figure emerging from under her blanket, followed by a smaller, rounder form, the form of a toddler. Almost crying with relief, he ran to Magpie's side and lifted both girls into his arms. Magpie looked into his eyes and saw they were red with tears. Big Hawk strode out of the camp carrying the girls. Magpie shrank into his arms, feeling his strength, and finally, after hours of stunned shock, she trembled and wept. Cricket, cradled on Magpie's stomach and in Big Hawk's arms, peered back over his bicep. But Magpie and Big Hawk did not look back. They could hear Black Kettle behind them, singing a death song of his own. Finally, the notes blended with the wind until Magpie wondered if she still heard Black Kettle. Perhaps the sound she heard was the wind, also in mourning, weeping and singing over those who remained.

Chapter Four

━━

Sand Creek, 1864

BLACK KETTLE WANDERED through his camp. He looked around in a daze; his heart heavy with shock; his feet moved of their own accord. A large fire smoldered at the center of the camp. Occasionally, black smoke erupted in large billows as the fire found something new to burn. Black Kettle knew the flames had consumed everything the Cheyennes had ever used in their daily lives, in their spiritual rituals, in their dances, or on the hunt. All was destroyed. He could see the charred remains of buffalo robes, cooking pots, a small brass kettle, a saddle. Colorful glass beads, likely from fancy moccasins or a baby's cradleboard, polished by the flames, glowed hot amid the embers. His way of life and that of his people had been obliterated. Black Kettle wondered if the Cheyennes would ever seek to own possessions again. Now that the traditional wintering ground around Sand Creek was profaned, would his people become ghosts, roaming the earth in search of a home?

As Black Kettle drifted, he came upon corpses mutilated beyond recognition. Women had been gunned down, babies killed in their arms. Very few corpses were those of men. "Why is it that the youngest and most vulnerable die first?" he asked, imploring the wind and the grasses to hear his anguish. The grasses swayed, rustling in the wind. Black Kettle dared to hope that Medicine Woman Later had survived. Again Black Kettle spoke to the wind, "Where is she? Where is my wife? I could not protect her. Perhaps you, Brother Wind, kept her safe?" Glancing around at the bodies on the ground he added, "I could not protect her. I could not protect them." As he searched for Medicine Woman Later, feelings of anguish and sorrow approached him from behind and stalked him at his side. Black Kettle spoke to his sorrow, "Leave me. I have no wish to feel anything right now. I am not ready to mourn," and he felt the emotion step away from him. After a few more paces Black Kettle recognized White Antelope, his body contorted below the lodgepole. Only by the distinctive markings on White Antelope's leggings could Black Kettle tell that the body belonged to his dear friend. White Antelope's face had been completely hacked away in the scalping. At the sight of his friend, Black Kettle felt his body collapse with grief. He was no longer able to keep his emotions at bay. He knelt beside White Antelope. As Black Kettle sang over White Antelope, sorrow and anguish took up residence in the empty pit of Black Kettle's stomach. Black Kettle did not welcome the emotions, but bowed in acceptance. He knew that it was right to carry sorrow with him. He knew that anguish would never leave him. This sadness had come to stay.

Black Kettle finished singing. He rose, stood straight, and looked around the camp. As he viewed the disaster, he was flooded with memories. He remembered the camps of his childhood. He remembered the creeks and rivers of his youth. He remembered the time before the *ve'ho'e* came and how the prophet Motse'eoeve, Sweet Medicine, had spoken to him in a vision.

Then the waters had run clear, gurgling and laughing as the bands of the tribe gathered for summer rituals and winter foraging. Black Kettle saw ponies grazing in the tall grasses in the upper river lands. He saw the young boys play running games, driving and steering the pony herd as they might buffalo. The boys practiced diligently for the day when they would go on the hunt and provide meat for the band. He saw younger children flocking from tipi to tipi in large groups, lured by the scent of skillet bread frying in buffalo fat. He saw older boys shooting arrows, wrestling, and honing their skills as warriors. He saw older men in small groups talking outside tipi door flaps and telling stories. He saw girls and young women working with their mothers and aunts, scraping hides, curing meat, and sewing large skins into tipis. The women worked, often with babies tightly wrapped in swaddling furs strapped to their backs. The infants were carried in extravagantly beaded cradleboards, testaments to the care and love lavished on the youngest of the band.

He remembered the many battles and raids he had fought and led as a younger man. Black Kettle remembered thrusting his spear into the ground, taking a stand, and fighting. He guarded his band with his life, ready to die to keep his family safe.

Since his youth, warfare had changed. He remembered the first time he saw the ve'ho'e in their creaking, ponderous wagons, loaded down with heavy goods and furniture. The wagons scarred deep ruts into the land. The wagon trails were easy to follow and settlers' horses even easier to steal. At first the ve'ho'e were unorganized and there were not that many of them. Raiding horses was a simple affair. Too simple. Warfare, which had been a seasonal occurrence, usually to secure horses or winter food stocks, became a way of life. Instead of going out to raid, Black Kettle and his men stayed home and defended their hunting lands from white incursions. The ve'ho'e came to them and they kept on coming. Nothing seemed to deter them and their numbers only increased.

As Black Kettle reflected, his gaze fell on a circular area near the edge of the camp. He remembered that the Cheyennes had a Sun Dance the summer of Big Hawk's first year. At the time of the summer solstice the men of the band rebuilt the traditional medicine lodge.

The men placed a tall, straight-forked lodgepole in the center of a large circular arbor. This pole was cut from a large, strong tree that grew straight and tall. The arbor was then covered with willow branches. These provided shade.

In the fork of the lodgepole the men placed prayer cloths, long pieces of material infused with the prayers of the People. Black Kettle danced so that the prayers on the lodgepole were released and renewed the tribe.

On the appointed day Black Kettle stripped himself of most of his clothing and all his gear. He wore simple trade cloth over his loins and covering his buttocks. Before he entered the sacred space of the medicine lodge, Medicine Woman Later purified him with a bouquet of smoking sage, passing the fragrant bundle up and down over his body several times. After Medicine Woman Later purified him he went to his painter who painted his body. Only then did he enter the medicine lodge with his painter and fellow dancers. He danced to the sacred songs for three days without food or drink. His thirst was unbearable in the dry summer heat. The dancers' families were careful not to flaunt any water in front of them. It was disrespectful. Gradually, his mind sank into the timeless space of the medicine lodge and into communing with Ma'heo'o, the Creator. He could not tell if he was dreaming or awake.

On the third day the vision he sought came to him. His mind cleared and he saw standing before him the great prophet, Motse'eoeve, Sweet Medicine. Motse'eoeve spoke. "These new people with pale skin and strange ways are the people of my prophecy. They will not return to their lands. They are here to stay and there are many of them, too many for the Cheyennes to fight. You, Black Kettle, a wise and thoughtful man, must lead your people down a hard path. You were a warrior but you are destined to become a great peace chief. To save your people you must compromise. Compromise so that you and your band will survive. For this you will be reviled and your family will suffer." And then Motse'eoeve left him. Black Kettle came out of the medicine lodge renewed and contemplative.

After his visitation from Sweet Medicine, Black Kettle realized that the only way his nephew could grow up without fear would be to make a deliberate, constructive peace with the ve'ho'e. To this task he committed himself. Black Kettle put aside his weapons of war. The elders of his band noticed his seriousness and respected his wishes. Since that time how many treaty negotiations had he led? How many tribal counsels had he sat through? How many times had he argued that the Cheyennes, the fiercest warriors on the plains, must put away their weapons and make a lasting peace? Had he been wrong to bring the tribe's chiefs together to sign the peace treaty? He had met his tribesmen gathered in a large oak grove. The meeting lasted for days. The men had argued in a seemingly endless fashion. Finally, Black Kettle lent his voice to the deliberations. He spoke eloquently of his vision during Big Hawk's first-year Sun Dance. "I will sign the treaty. I will make war no more. I will raid no more. We must learn to live in peace with our white brothers." Others had scoffed at him. They had said, "You will not save your people by signing. The only language the ve'ho'e understand is that of violence and war." Had he been wrong to sign the treaty? Was his vision from Motse'eoeve a hoax? Was it a cosmic joke? No, it could not be. Motse'eoeve's prophecies were true. The ve'ho'e were here to stay and his people must adapt. If he were to live his life again, he would make the same decisions.

In that moment of clarity Black Kettle saw his wife. She lay quite still, her legs in a runner's stance, as if in flight. She was riddled with bullets but by some miracle she was still breathing. She was alive. "Do not take me from this death place. I will die here with my people," she whispered, her eyes fading as she spoke. Black Kettle examined her body, counting the nine bullets buried in her flesh. Then he answered her. "You will die with your people, but not today. These bullets are bad but not fatal. You are a medicine woman. You must teach me how to heal you." She was shaking from the cold and the loss of blood. "A blanket," she whispered. Black Kettle looked around. A few yards away he noticed Sage Woman's blanket, warm and alive, even on this bitter day. He crossed the space to Sage Woman's body and knelt by her side. "Big Hawk has your children. Magpie and Cricket are safe. I am sorry to take this special blanket from you, Sage Woman. Surely, you and White Antelope can do without it in the next life." He looked around. "You will have much good company to keep you warm. May I have it? Medicine Woman Later needs it now." He removed the blanket from Sage Woman's body, and running back to his wife he covered Medicine Woman Later's body with it. Medicine Woman Later moaned and winced in pain as he hoisted her over his shoulder. With Medicine Woman Later draped over him, he walked away from the devastated camp, now smoldering under the vast and endless sky.

Chapter Five

~~

Fort Cobb, 1868

ROSS POLK TOOK a soft cloth from an instrument case on his cot and shined his prized trumpet. He glanced dismissively at the dented military bugle lying beside the bag. It was a good thing he had brought his own instruments with him. He had just arrived at Fort Cobb in Indian Territory a few hours earlier. Playing a bugle was not what he had planned for his future. He wanted to teach music but not too many folks could afford lessons after the war.

"Hey, Bugle Boy," a voice from outside his tent commanded, "come play us a tune." Ross Polk stood up from his army-issue cot, his thin body a pencil-like shadow against the tent's canvas. How did the speaker know he was the new bugle player for the Seventh Cavalry? "Who's asking?" he called out.

"A commanding officer. Now get out here and play Colonel Hazen and myself a nice tune. Know any Irish songs?" Ross gulped down his coffee. He hesitated and almost reached for his bugle but then changed his mind. He grabbed his trumpet and stepped outside. He gasped at the temperature as he joined the rakish-looking officer outside the tent.

Even though Custer was of lesser rank, he spoke first. "Name's Custer, Lieutenant Colonel George Armstrong Custer, hero of the Civil War. Perhaps you've heard tell of me. I've come from Camp Supply to visit my old friend Colonel Hazen here." At those words Ross noticed a flicker of tension pass between the two men. Clearly they were not old friends. "He tells me you're a good horn player. I do enjoy a good tune now and then." Custer laughed harshly. Ross didn't dare join in the laughter. Ross noticed that Colonel

Hazen had flinched at Custer's wild introduction of himself. Custer had barely acknowledged Hazen's presence even though Hazen was his superior. Ross was surprised that Hazen did not confront Custer. Perhaps, Ross reasoned to himself, Hazen had decided to wait until a more suitable time when he was alone with Custer. Custer was known throughout the army as the most flamboyant of the officer class. He dressed extravagantly and always traveled with a brass band, which, in addition to providing entertainment for the men, also played during cavalry charges. Perhaps Hazen realized that confronting Custer was like taming a wild horse; one had to do it with care.

Custer's demand put Ross in a delicate position. The cold air would likely freeze the trumpet valves shut, potentially ruining his prized instrument.

"I would greatly enjoy playing for you but this weather is not good for instruments," he responded.

Custer snorted. "Young man, I've commanded plenty of campaigns. I know when to play an instrument and when not to play. Now . . . play on."

"Can I at least invite you into my tent where it is warmer?"

Custer hesitated at the bold request. During his pause, Hazen took the opportunity to assert his authority. "You have my permission to step inside the tent."

"Thank you, sir." Ross turned back into the tent but not before he noticed that Custer tried to force his way ahead of Colonel Hazen. Hazen stood his ground and, without saying a word, stepped in front of Custer. Only at the last moment did Custer give way.

Once back inside the tent Ross centered his feet solidly on the ground, raised the trumpet to his mouth, pursed his lips, and blew some long slow notes into the instrument to warm it. He fingered the valves, making sure they weren't frozen.

First quietly, then building the sound, he drew air through his nose before blowing it through the trumpet in an attempt to warm the air. As he raised the trumpet to his lips he still had no idea what to play. To his surprise, instead of playing a stirring solo, a quiet melody issued from his trumpet. It evoked loneliness and matched his mood. Perhaps, Ross reflected as he played, this piece came to him because this was truly how he felt. The vast landscapes of Indian Territory made him feel small and vulnerable. At the end of the piece, the notes seemed to linger in the cold still air, lending melancholy to the already sad piece.

Custer's response ended the mood created by Ross and his trumpet. "Hey, he's good. I didn't know the army could recruit such good brass players. But son, you've got to play something more lively. Play a tune, a jig, something to keep us entertained. Where are you from, boy?"

"I grew up in a small town on the Chesapeake Bay, in Maryland."

"Humph." Custer sounded skeptical. "Marylanders. We never knew whose side they were on. North or South, boy?"

"North. I'm from northern Maryland. Chestertown, to be exact. My older brother fought for the Union," Ross responded.

"You grew up on the bay?" Colonel Hazen asked.

"Yes, sir, do you know it? My family once owned land along the Chester River."

"The Chester River? That's tobacco country, isn't it? You grew up there and you didn't own slaves? Everyone owned slaves along the Chesapeake. You're telling me your family fought for the North and you didn't own slaves?" There was a note of incredulity in Hazen's voice.

"That's true, sir. My people owned slaves but not my immediate family."

"What happened? Your people sink into debt like so many slavers?" Hazen's questions were sharp and intended to put Ross, now perceived as a Southerner, in his place.

Ross figured he might as well fully explain his family's humble position.

"My grandfather was a tobacco planter. He owned slaves. After he died, my father inherited the plantation but it was all farmed out. We couldn't even grow chickweed. We didn't need slaves anymore. We couldn't afford them. Pa had to sell—slaves, land, the house—almost everything. After that I grew up working out."

"Working out?" Hazen inquired.

"That's what we say when our farms can't support us. We end up hiring ourselves out. I worked in the fields some, but mostly on the wharves and on the bay. My family—we're watermen now. Crabbing, oystering, and fishing mainly."

"So you didn't grow up thinking you owned the world by owning slaves?" Hazen questioned.

"No, sir," Ross answered. "The wharves and the water taught me to work and also that there aren't that many differences between people, when it comes right down to it. I worked with slaves, freeborn, poor whites, and even some students from Washington College. That's nearby, you know. Folks come to Chestertown from all over, even Europe. Captains from England sail their trading ships up the Chester River. I worked with them, too. It is a small town but folks know us."

Ross was proud of his hometown. The houses along the wharves were substantial, built of brick and stone. The town supported a college. It was prosperous. Some had sided with the North, most with the South, but the townspeople had not turned on one another. The town's location had protected it from being shelled. Unlike so many other towns just south of the Mason-Dixon line, Chestertown had escaped the Civil War unscathed.

"Where did you learn to play?" Hazen's question interrupted Ross's thoughts. "You have remarkable talent."

"My mother was a piano teacher; that is, until she married. Sometimes she taught students from the college. She taught me theory and notes on the piano. I taught myself to play trumpet. There's not much to do in Chestertown after the working day is over." Ross smiled ruefully.

Hazen smiled back at him. "Work has taken me to Washington and I've been on the bay a few times, crossing from Annapolis to the Eastern Shore. It's a lovely place, still seems wild even though it's been settled for over two hundred years," he mused.

Now Custer addressed Ross. "So you were raised on the water. A real wharf rat."

"Yes, sir." For a moment Ross's pride turned to something deeper and darker as melancholy took hold again. He missed the sounds of water playfully slapping against the boat's sides as she cut through the waves. He missed the familiar rocking of wood on water, sails extended on a full run, dancing with the wind. He missed the close, protected feeling of the forests, oak and pine, coming right down to water's edge in the many coves and inlets of the bay. He missed fishing for rockfish and hauling up the heavy crab pots. He missed sailing down to Virginia, circling the bay's many islands, and dredging for oysters before the winter ice set in. As he breathed in the cold air, he missed the comforting gray-green waters shimmering in the hazy eastern sun.

"This here's not country for folks who like water," Custer observed. "But give it time, son. You can see forever out here. The wind causes the grass to wave and ripple just like water. And the sunsets out here are incomparable."

Ross was taken aback. Custer, usually so loud and verbose, had a bit of poetry in him.

To hide his confusion, Ross turned back to the finely wrought black leather case on his cot. He picked up the fine cotton cloth with fibers as soft as silk and began polishing and cleaning the brass. Hazen admired the way Ross took such care with his instrument.

"That's a beautiful trumpet. You must have brought it with you from Chestertown. Finding an instrument like that out here on the prairie is like stumbling across a piano. Believe me, it's been done. Folks get out here thinking they'll establish high culture, but their draft animals get so tired and worn down that they pitch everything, right out the back of the wagon. One of my men claims to have found a small pump organ, brought all the way from Vermont, just dumped beside a trail."

"Do you play any other instruments?" Custer abruptly asked.

"I also play violin, sir."

Custer's gruff, loud demeanor returned. "A fiddle!" he exclaimed with excitement. "We've got ourselves a fiddle player."

"Excuse me, sir, but I must tell you I don't play the fiddle." He tucked his trumpet under one arm. "I'm a classically trained musician. I'll play bugle calls for the cavalry but would prefer to play my trumpet and violin. Let me show you my violin. I worked two summers to pay for this violin." Ross sat down on his cot, reached under, and gingerly placed another beautifully crafted instrument case on his knees. Hazen's eyes widened at the lovely wood grain and fine craftsmanship of Ross's violin. Ross picked up the violin with great care. His slim fingers grasped the bow and he tucked the violin under his chin, preparing to play a tune, mindful that it needed to suit Custer's demands.

Custer, oblivious to the beauty of the instrument, responded with anger.

"Now look here. We'll have none of that, young man. Not on my watch. When I need a tune to put a spring in my step and get my boys moving, I don't need Bach and Beethoven and whatever it is that you just played on that horn of yours. Give me some military music. Something we can march to. Something we can fight to. Something that gets us in the mood for blood." Ross felt like rolling his eyes at Custer's rant, but he held his countenance.

"Since you mentioned Beethoven, have you considered Beethoven's symphony known as *Wellington's Victory*?

"Huh?" Custer was taken aback. Hazen hid a smirk under his moustache. It was good to see Custer set on his heels.

Ross explained: "Some performances include gunfire. It starts with a snare drum and a wonderful trumpet solo. You like brass, right? It has charges and volleys. It's very inspiring."

"Gunfire is good," Custer remarked. "I haven't heard of a piece called *Wellington's Victory*. Can you play it? We could fire off our carbines at the appropriate moment."

"It starts with a trumpet solo and it includes a large brass section. I could work with the band. We won't be able to play the piece in its entirety but depending on the level of musicianship we might perform the brass music for you. We could make the carbines a central part of the music." Ross mentioned gunfire again. "I think you'd like it. It's very militaristic and dramatic."

Colonel Hazen smiled inwardly and made a mental note. The boy had potential. He was smart and could talk to his superiors, diplomatically disagreeing while sticking to his points.

Hazen's thoughts were interrupted when three soldiers made their presence known outside the tent. Two Osage scouts stood by. The soldiers saluted smartly. The Indians stood without moving, their eyes fixed on Custer's long hair. One soldier addressed both Custer and Hazen.

"We've spotted a camp. It's along the Washita. It's small, just a handful of tipis, not more than fifty or so. We believe we can take it."

Custer quickly answered, "A small band of savages? That sounds promising. Is this small band big enough to make newspaper headlines? It can't be too small, you know. Then what's the point?"

"Perhaps, sir, since so many of your men are recent recruits, practicing on this small band would season them for engagement on a larger scale," suggested the soldier. "We have not seen any evidence of larger groups in the area."

Custer considered the information before demanding, "How far from here?"

"About ten miles."

"How did you find it?" Custer asked.

"We followed a game trail, sir. It looks like the Indians were tracking game. The Osage scouts said the Indians had killed a couple of deer. The trail led us straight to the camp. It looks to be Cheyenne." The soldier hesitated. "There is a white flag flying in the camp."

Hazen startled. "If that's Cheyenne and if there's a white flag, that would be Black Kettle's band."

Custer, knowing that a white flag meant the camp was peaceful, nonetheless retorted, "Why should I pay attention to white flags? They are meaningless."

Hazen raised his eyebrows at Custer and responded, "Black Kettle's band is peaceful. He is the peace chief for the entire Cheyenne people, and he will not make war. He was a signer of the Medicine Lodge Treaty. He and his wife survived the massacre at Sand Creek four years ago. It is said she took nine bullets that day."

Custer shrugged.

Hazen noticed he wasn't making much headway with Custer, who seemed unconcerned that Black Kettle was not a war chief. Hazen decided to change tactics and appealed to Custer's apparent need for publicity. "That massacre at Sand Creek, and that's what it was—a massacre—received horrible press. Horrible press," he repeated for emphasis. "The East Coast papers were highly critical. If that's Black Kettle's camp, you'll want to pick another group. You'll want to avoid attacking Black Kettle. He's worked for many years to keep his young men peaceful. He wants peace with whites. His reputation as a peacemaker is well-known and highly regarded."

Now Hazen had Custer's attention. Custer fell silent for a while and then, seemingly, his mind made up, he turned to Hazen. "Have his warriors kept the peace or have they broken it?"

"The warriors in his band have kept the peace. His band has not attacked whites in years. Even after Sand Creek his band did not attack," Hazen responded, irritation creeping into his voice. He was not used to having his authority questioned. "Other Cheyennes were enraged at what happened to Black Kettle's band and sought retribution."

Custer, oblivious to Hazen's growing irritation, continued his questioning. "So other Cheyennes, they have not kept the peace? Isn't that right?"

"You know as well as I do the Cheyennes have a council of forty-four chiefs. As a peace chief, Black Kettle does not control all Cheyennes. He can only speak for those in his small band," Hazen countered. "And no one controls the Dog Soldiers," he added.

"What you are telling me is that not all Cheyennes are peaceful. So who cares if Black Kettle signs peace agreements and treaties? If he can't control his warriors, if the Cheyenne Dog Soldiers are making war on us—and you just said they are—then that says to me the Cheyenne nation is making war on us."

Hazen was alarmed. "The Cheyennes are hardly a nation. They are more of a loose confederation of small bands each going their own way. The only time they gather for more than a few days is during the winter months and also during the Sun Dance in summer. I'm telling you, I've worked with Black Kettle. He wants peace. His men have not attacked whites. Other Cheyennes, yes. Dog soldiers, yes. But not Black Kettle's group. You should not attack Black Kettle's camp."

Custer stared at Colonel Hazen. "With all due respect, sir, I am surprised you used such language with me. The Union Army just defeated one confederation. A lot of my boys died in that war. Now I guess it's time to defeat another confederation. General Sheridan sent me here to fight Indians. I am under direct orders not to differentiate one from the other. Sheridan cleared out all the Indians up north. Now we're getting rid of them down here. You're asking my soldiers and these scouts to figure out the difference between one Cheyenne group and another? That's crazy."

Ross noticed that Hazen was close to losing his cool with Custer. Hazen's response was delivered in measured tones. "Your Osage scouts can easily identify one Plains Indian encampment from the next. Black Kettle always flies a white flag. As your commanding officer, I am ordering you to figure out whose camp that is and why the white flag is flying before you attack."

Custer had had enough. The time for talking was through. "You are my commanding officer, Colonel Hazen, but we aren't back East. Communication lines, as you know, don't work out here. I was sent here to fight and secure land for white settlers. I was told directly by General Sheridan to kill all Indians I came across. If you had your way, soon all the Indians would fly white flags and, according to you, I wouldn't be able to attack any of them. What rot! I'll return to Camp Supply tomorrow morning. From there I will muster my men and move out." He addressed Ross: "Best get your things together, boy, because you are coming with me."

Custer turned to the scouts and soldiers. "When we get to Camp Supply tell the boys to kill the dogs. I don't want any barking and yapping to give away my approach. You are dismissed." Custer could not direct his anger at Hazen so he turned to vent his rage on Ross. "And you . . . bugle and fiddle boy, you've got one night to learn my favorite classic Irish drinking song." His voice lingered on the word *classic* as if to taunt Ross. "It's the highly melodic, inspiring, and dramatic 'Garryowen.' That's what I want to hear when we march out tomorrow morning."

Ross sighed. "Garryowen" was a tune for layabouts and lowlifes who drank all day. Not exactly Beethoven. Perhaps he could play a variation on "Garryowen," make it a bit more complicated and musically interesting.

Hazen shook his head, his anger now palpable. "We may be living out here at the edges of the earth but we are still in communication with the East. I'll ask you one last time to reconsider. Do your homework; find out if that camp is indeed Black Kettle's. If it is, move away from it."

Custer, now completely flustered, responded angrily, "These are not white brothers in gray. Hell, they're not even Negroes. At least Negroes fight like men. These are Indians. I don't need to do homework here. Back East we were fighting white men, worthy enemies. That is not the case here."

Hazen had worked and lived in the East. He knew the military didn't pay much attention to insubordination in the West. Custer had been given free rein. He had many loyal, well-trained, and heavily armed men under his command. Hazen stroked his beard. "If that is your attitude, then you will forgive me for saying that if disaster strikes, you had it coming." Custer stared at Hazen and wheeled away, almost ripping the flap off the tent's door as he left. He yelped as he stubbed his toe hard on the tent pole and left limping and muttering.

Hazen looked hard at Ross. "I'm to meet with Black Kettle tonight. God

45

only knows what I will say to him. Custer is determined to shed innocent blood. Peaceful men, women, and children will die. As one of Custer's men, you will be drawn into this conflict. My boy, your life and your music might never recover. In this case, there may be nothing a mere trumpeter can do. But do what you can, son. Try to spare the innocent." Hazen turned abruptly and left. Ross, shaken by Hazen's words, peered outside the tent into the snow. He shivered, the differences between "Garryowen" and Beethoven diminishing as he watched the whipping snow. The wind howled a mournful dirge.

Chapter Six

Washita, 1868

IT SEEMED BIG hawk saw everything. His eyes were always on her, watching her, teasing her. Magpie ignored his looks and turned to Medicine Woman Later. "Nahaa'e," Magpie said, "I need to tell you about the tracks. I saw boots, wagon wheels, horses. Many of them."

Medicine Woman Later, distracted by Big Hawk's taunting of Magpie, barely heard the girl. She frowned at her nephew. It seemed all he wanted to do was quarrel with Magpie. Big Hawk should maintain silence around Magpie. He should never address her, at least not directly. Where were his manners? Perhaps he thought since they weren't blood related he could tease her. But this was not the Cheyenne way. Perhaps she should ask Black Kettle to speak with Big Hawk. His behavior toward Magpie risked his reputation and the honor of the family.

Ever since the massacre at Sand Creek Medicine Woman Later had doted on Magpie and Cricket, watching over the spirited young girls as closely as she could. She had tried to train the girls as Sage Woman and White Antelope would have wanted. She had grown to love Magpie and Cricket as daughters. Medicine Woman Later's attentiveness meant she had seen Big Hawk's awkward attempts to engage Magpie in conversation, often resorting to teasing when he could think of nothing to say. She had also seen him sorting through his blankets, fingering the finest wool among them. Did he intend to approach Magpie? Medicine Woman Later could not have been more pleased. Magpie was intelligent and strong. She was quick to learn and always helpful. Magpie was also a diligent worker and one who kept the traditional ways. Sage Woman's early training had paid off.

"Hey Magpie. When you decide to get serious about hunting, let me know. I'll teach you everything." Big Hawk's taunts invaded Medicine Woman Later's thoughts. Medicine Woman Later sighed in exasperation. She decided to help Big Hawk in his wooing of Magpie. Chasing Magpie around lodgepoles? Taunting her instead of respectfully wooing her like a lover? This was no way to win the heart of a young Cheyenne woman.

"Big Hawk, you are too bothered by ve'ho'e women who are not allowed to hunt," observed Medicine Woman Later. "We have many women in our tribe who can hunt as well as men. Cheyenne women can fight, too. You know the story of Lightning Woman. She fought alongside her brother, led our tribe into battle, and counted many coups. Perhaps someday you and Magpie will fight together and count coups. She is strong, fast, and brave. We need women like her now. You should also remember Cheyenne tradition. Do not flout the rules of behavior. You must not speak to a young woman like that. You must maintain dignity and respect toward all Cheyenne women. You know our ways. Keep them."

Big Hawk retreated under his aunt's instructions. He realized his mistake and when he spoke again to Magpie, his voice was gentle. "You are quick to learn and you've trained your ponies well. As long as you can bring home game and keep a cooking pot full of meat, you will be a great hunter. I am sorry if I offended you. I will not speak to you again." As he said these words he thought to himself, *Though you will not need to hunt. Let me hunt for you and keep your cooking pot full of meat.* He did not say these words. Instead, he moved to a stack of blankets and began to sort through them. He fingered each one, assessing the quality of the wool and looking at the design. Which one would most please Magpie? Which blanket should he use to cover them both and speak to her of love? She was quick and, in some ways, fierce. At the very bottom of the pile of blankets a strong striped pattern stood out. The blanket looked familiar but he couldn't place it in his memory. He gathered the blanket and glanced at Magpie. She turned toward him. He smiled a shy smile at her over his shoulder. Then, lifting the tipi's door flap, he disappeared out into the wind.

"Where do you think he's going with that blanket?" Magpie asked her *nahaa'e*.

Medicine Woman Later was intrigued that Magpie and Big Hawk could not remember the blanket. It was distinctive. Medicine Woman Later had saved it for the last four years, carefully tucking it into her household travois as the band had followed the game trails. It was the only item she had from before the massacre at Sand Creek, the only thing she had to remind her of her dearest friend, Sage Woman. Should she tell Big Hawk about the blanket? Perhaps that story should wait until later. Perhaps she should wait to see if Big Hawk indeed intended to court Magpie.

Medicine Woman Later answered, "Big Hawk is old enough to hunt, to provide meat for a family. He is old enough to court a girl and marry."

Magpie was startled. Of course she knew Big Hawk would marry. But so soon? Magpie knew he should never and would never choose her. She was too familiar. Since her parents died, Magpie and Big Hawk had grown up practically in the same tipi. Tribal custom prohibited any interaction between brothers and sisters, even those who weren't blood related. *He probably doesn't know what to do about me any more than I know what to do about him*, she mused. *Maybe he thinks of me like a little sister.* Lately, he either avoided her completely, as a proper brother should, or teased and made fun of her, breaking all dignified rules of conduct. He should not approach her. But was Big Hawk her brother? He was not of her family. Although close to Medicine Woman Later and Black Kettle, she had not been adopted by them. If her parents had not been killed, he could have courted her. How respectful of tribal customs should she be? When the world seems to be falling apart who keeps traditional ways? Perhaps it's enough to simply survive. Her questions about Big Hawk made her feel shy, awkward, and ill at ease around him.

She closed her eyes and remembered her parents. She wished her parents hadn't died at Sand Creek. She wished she was from another band so that Big Hawk would notice her at the dances. She regretted that he was so comfortable with her. He should be a little more cautious, more like the other young men who watched her from a distance. Then she answered her own regrets. "Big Hawk has watched over you like a protective older brother. Yes, he teases, but he can also be tender. He protected you on the day your world ended. He understands you and knows your past.

Everything with Big Hawk will be good no matter his intentions. Put Big Hawk out of your mind. You have more important things to think about."

Magpie again tried to get and keep Medicine Woman Later's attention. "*Nahaa'e,* I saw tracks today. White man's tracks. Many of them. There is an army nearby. It is on the move." Once again, it seemed as though Medicine Woman Later did not hear Magpie's words. Was she absorbed in her own thoughts?

"Magpie, I need your help." Medicine Woman Later looked her over. Medicine Woman Later thought Magpie, too, needed to be clued in. If Big Hawk was indeed getting ready to court Magpie, the girl should be prepared. "Wash your face." Medicine Woman Later chided Magpie as if speaking to a young child: "You are Cheyenne. You are of Black Kettle's band. Our people do not walk around with grease and dirt on our faces. You are old enough to keep yourself clean." Magpie was taken aback. She was clean; her face freshly washed every day. You would think that her people did nothing but bathe in the river all day, so important was washing.

Magpie knew she must obey Medicine Woman Later, but urgency overrode training and pushed her to try again to speak to Medicine Woman Later. "*Nahaa'e,* I need you to listen to me now." Magpie's voice rose with agitation. "You listen to the wind and rain; please hear my words. There are many *ve'ho'e* around. We are in trouble."

Medicine Woman Later shook her head. "It's not possible. They will not attack our band again. Not after Sand Creek. Not after all the many negotiations and treaties my husband signed. I will not hear it, Magpie." Medicine Woman Later bent her head over her cooking pot.

Magpie sighed deeply in defeat. She knew she had tried. Perhaps she should try to talk with Black Kettle when he returned. Catching the older woman looking at her from beneath her lashes as she stirred the cooking pot, Magpie finally obeyed her. Going outside, she scooped up some newly fallen snow. She vigorously scrubbed her face. Then she came back to the lodge, her skin glowing with her efforts. Sticking her face back in through the door flap, she presented herself to Medicine Woman Later. Medicine Woman Later glanced at Magpie and smiled her approval. She observed, "We need more wood for the fire. Cooking after the successful hunt has used up my firewood. Your sharp eyes can help me. Come walk with me to the river." Magpie threw a protective blanket over her shoulders and followed the path to the river with Medicine Woman Later.

As she stepped from the tipi with Medicine Woman Later, Magpie noticed the air clearing. Light, large snowflakes fell quickly, covering the ground and the women's footprints. As they walked the winds shifted, bringing a sudden drop in temperature. The snowflakes condensed, becoming smaller and harder. Magpie shivered and drew her blanket tightly around her shoulders. As she looked up, she saw Big Hawk standing in the bushes. Draped over his shoulder was a richly hued blanket, its bold stripes standing out against the rounded shapes and white shadows of the snow drifting around him. He stood silently, watching her come down the path with his aunt. As they walked past him he turned toward them, shifting his stance and following their movements with his body. She could feel his eyes on her back. Magpie knew she was not to look over her shoulder at him. What on earth was he doing? He couldn't possibly be courting her. She couldn't help herself and she glanced back quickly. He was still watching her, and when he saw her turn toward him he raised his hand, an open hand, beckoning her to watch and wait for him. As he raised his hand she was drawn to the wool blanket wrapped around his shoulders. *At least he intends to court me in the traditional way. He chose a good blanket*, she thought. *That one suits me.*

As Magpie walked with Medicine Woman Later to gather wood, she again tried to sort out her feelings for Big Hawk. She was surprised that Big Hawk meant to court her. How else to interpret his actions? He had chosen a beautiful blanket. He stood respectfully by the path. He gestured to her silently, asking her to meet him upon her return. Magpie knew the decision was hers. If she decided to receive his attentions she would stand beside him. He would wrap them both in his blanket and, standing under its comfort, speak to her, telling her why she should consent to have him as a husband. She shivered. This was such an odd time for courting. Why in the midst of an early cold winter would his mind turn to courtship? Why could he not have waited until the warmth of spring? Springtime is the proper courting time.

Magpie and Medicine Woman Later walked to their favorite stand of cottonwood trees. Here the snow was not as deep, and Magpie started to gather small sticks and branches for the fire. She broke fallen branches in two and placed them in a bundle to carry back to the lodge. The snap of the twigs mimicked the sound of the wind as it whipped through the trees. She looked around and saw that Medicine Woman Later had sat down. Since Medicine Woman Later hardly ever sat down, Magpie thought it best to wait, and she silently stood by the old woman's side as the elder adjusted her shawl, wrapping it tightly. As she crossed her arms, Medicine Woman Later began to rock back and forth. When Medicine Woman Later started rocking, Magpie knew what was coming next: the story of Sand Creek. Medicine Woman Later had told Magpie this story over and over, instructing her to commit it to memory because, "Someday, you will tell this story to your children."

After a few moments Medicine Woman Later stopped rocking and stood up. She sang to the four sacred directions: turning, pausing, and singing strongly into the wind. Then she sat down and looked at Magpie, reaching out to touch Magpie's forehead and cheek. When she spoke, she was filled with emotion. "I know you are angry and impatient because Black Kettle has tried to work with the *ve'ho'e*. I know you are angry and impatient with me because I cannot believe your story about the tracks. Surely, you are mistaken. You know that Black Kettle has gone to Fort Cobb to ask for protection from Colonel Hazen. Someday, you will take my place as a leader of the People. Someday, you and Big Hawk will walk down the path Black Kettle has cleared and you will make the decisions."

"Excuse me, Nahaa'e, but he will not find protection. I saw tracks today. I did, Nahaa'e. I did," Magpie insisted. When Medicine Woman Later remained silent, Magpie persisted, "Please listen. There were many horses, many wagon wheels. *Ve'ho'e* army men are here. They are here with their horses. They will kill us from their horses. We need to move toward the others along the Washita. Nahaa'e, please."

Instead of responding to her plea Medicine Woman Later said, "You, my wonderful Magpie, are still here. You and Cricket are well named. You are so small. Your stature is your grace. It has saved you. Your *heške* hid you under her blanket. The army men did not see you and there you stayed, as still as small birds hiding in a bush. You, Magpie, outwitted the eagle. I was shot nine times that day and thought that I too would die. Black Kettle watched from the sand bunkers, and when the soldiers left he came back looking for me. When he found me, he slung me over his shoulder and ran out onto the open prairie seeking refuge. Big Hawk found you and brought you out of that death place. Now we are here, in this new place by this new river, the Washita. We need to stop the killing. This bad story has to come to an end. Someday, if we cannot make the peace you, Magpie, will need to make a lasting peace with the *ve'ho'e.*"

Magpie listened respectfully, although her mind was in turmoil. She was certain that attempting to make a lasting peace with whites was a waste of time. Even though she disagreed, she silently repeated Medicine Woman Later's words.

For a long time, no one in the tribe had spoken of Sand Creek. But lately she had heard the story so much she did not know where her memory ended and the story began. "I will try to do as you want, Nahaa'e," she said softly, putting the old woman's mind at ease.

Medicine Woman Later stood up and once again sang to the four sacred directions. "Black Kettle should be home by now. Let's gather wood and get out of this storm before it gets any worse."

As they gathered wood, the cottonwood trees bent and swayed in the wind. The branches rattled against one another so much that it sounded as if the trees were playing drums. Magpie frowned. Was that a person swaying in the branches of the cottonwoods? What was she hearing? A lithe figure came through the grove, walking toward them.

Chapter Seven

~

Washita, 1868

MAGPIE SQUINTED INTO the snow, trying to see who was coming toward her. At first the figure looked like a shadow emerging from the trees. As it came closer the body took form. He moved like a well-muscled man, balanced and strong. Unlike many of the Plains tribal people he was not tall. He was a young man, about Big Hawk's age. His features were so fine he looked almost like a girl. Unlike Cheyenne men, who braided their hair tightly into three long plaits, he wore his hair tied on either side of his head, loosely bound with an otter tail on one side and wrapped in leather on the other. The young man carried a bow and had a large quiver of arrows on his back. He also had a small pistol that was tucked into a *ve'ho'e* man's belt strapped around his middle. A large silver hoop pierced his right ear and a small, flattened silver medallion wrapped around one of his long slim fingers, like a long, thin oval ring.

Magpie could not take her eyes off the silver. She wasn't used to seeing men in such finery and never while on a hunt. *Must be Kiowa*, she thought. *No other plainsmen would wear so much silver.* She whispered to Medicine Woman Later, "It is said you can always tell a Kiowa raiding party from as far away as the horizon because when they ride, flashes of silver glint in the sun."

Medicine Woman Later smiled in agreement. The silver on the young man suddenly reminded her of the *ve'ho'e* men's army buttons. They too liked to adorn themselves with shiny ornaments. Comparing Kiowa with the *ve'ho'e* army seemed ironic and she resisted making a comment to the young man, certain it would offend him.

"Greetings," he signaled to Medicine Woman Later, using the common Plains language. "My tribe, the Kiowa, call me Eonah-pah, Trailing the Enemy. I've been hunting for a few days and made camp just over the ridge. Can I camp with you tonight? I'd like to get out of the storm and share some stories."

Medicine Woman Later placed her bundle of wood on the ground, straightened to her full height, and with dignity signed back: "How was your hunt?"

The young man smiled ruefully. "I'm down to my last bit of dried meat."

Medicine Woman Later chortled. "We have fresh meat. Come to my camp. I'll make sure you are fed well."

As a chief's wife, Medicine Woman Later was expected to feed all those who came into the camp, friends and enemies alike. Since Medicine Woman Later enjoyed feeding people, this was not a burden to her.

"Our band is this way," Medicine Woman Later gestured. "Just up a bit from the river." Magpie and Medicine Woman Later picked up the wood they had gathered and walked with Eonah-pah back to their camp.

Big Hawk was still standing beside the pathway, silent in the tall rustling bushes as the wind wrapped his blanket around him. The blanket's rich colors stood out and even in the darkening light seemed to shiver and dance in the wind. Medicine Woman Later walked onward with determination but Eonah-pah shook his head in wonder and tapped Medicine Woman Later on the shoulder, asking, "Cheyenne men court in storms, during winter winds? Why not wait until warmer breezes blow? That's when a man should find a wife."

Medicine Woman Later signed in response: "The trouble with the *ve'ho'e* has turned our world around. When was the last time the Kiowa had a Sun Dance? We keep to the old ways as best we can. Sometimes we must make adjustments."

Magpie kept quiet but noticed how Big Hawk again turned toward her as she passed, tracing her movements with the direction of his body as he held out his hand to her. Instead of looking away immediately, she turned toward Big Hawk as she passed and let her eyes stray to his face. She looked directly at him. Her sharp, dark eyes were wide with surprise. Big Hawk read the consternation in her face as well as a hint of welcome. Now it was clear he was courting her. He smiled reassurance at her. His eyes twinkled with humor. He seemed to say, *Why are you so surprised, Magpie?* Magpie hesitated on the path, letting Medicine Woman Later and Eonah-pah venture ahead of her. She wanted to stay with Big Hawk and let him cover her with his courting blanket. She wanted to hear him tell her why she should become his wife. However, the situation was urgent. Big Hawk and his courting blanket would have to wait a little bit longer. She made a gesture of apology toward Big Hawk then turned to hurry and catch up to Eonah-pah and Medicine Woman Later. As she came closer to the camp Magpie heard the sound of drums. The celebration of a good hunt had begun.

Eonah-pah and Magpie settled into Medicine Woman Later's comfortable lodge. Eonah-pah dipped his spoon into the stew. As he ate he signed, "I've come across horse tracks, horses with horseshoes, many of them. Wagons too. They are heading this direction. I don't think you are safe here. You should move your camp nearer to the others."

Magpie read his signing hands before speaking and signing to Medicine Woman Later, "That's what I've been trying to tell you, Nahaa'e. We are not safe. There are army men, lots of them, on horses. I also saw the tracks today. The paths through the snow and ice are worn smooth from their boots."

Eonah-pah, eager to eat, took another bite of food before adding, "I confirm this young woman's warnings. The situation is dire. Can you call the People together and move your camp?"

Medicine Woman Later looked at Magpie and in her glance she let Magpie know she was sorry she had not listened earlier. "It would be nice," Medicine Woman Later agreed with Eonah-pah, "to camp closer to the other tribes. We would like to camp closer to the Kiowas, Apaches, and our old friends the Arapahos, but we are not welcome. We must camp away from the others. Since my husband, Black Kettle, refuses to fight the *ve'ho'e*, others, even other Cheyennes, do not want to camp with us. We are not wanted."

Eonah-pah suggested, his hands moving gracefully, "Then perhaps you should move to the fort. Ask for protection from Colonel Hazen. The Kiowas think Hazen is sympathetic to Indians."

Magpie interjected, slapping her hands twice for emphasis as she signed, "I would not put much stock in a *ve'ho'e's* words. Better to move closer to the tribes."

Medicine Woman Later sighed. She knew why Magpie felt the way she did. Should she tell the young Kiowa how she also distrusted the *ve'ho'e*? Should she tell him about what happened at Sand Creek? For the longest time Medicine Woman Later had not spoken of the horror she experienced that day. Once she started talking, she could hardly stop. She did not know when she should share the story and when she should keep quiet. Her story was like so many other stories. Every tribe had experienced this brutality. Why should her story be retold to those outside her family, outside her band?

"Perhaps you are right," she gestured to Eonah-pah. "Perhaps we should move closer to the fort. You are welcome to rest here. My husband, Black Kettle, is at Fort Cobb now, talking with Colonel Hazen. I cannot move the camp until he returns. I will speak to him after he comes home." She turned to Magpie. "I'm sorry I did not hear you earlier. I did not want to and my mind was on other things. I understand now. I'll do what I can."

Chapter Eight

~

Fort Cobb, 1868

COLONEL HAZEN PACED around his office, trying to control his temper. He was incensed by Custer's audacity, his pushy ways and his bragging. *How did Custer ever get through officer training*, Hazen wondered. He knew the answer before he completed the thought. The war had required all men, even those with questionable character. Hazen had served long enough to know that in wartime some men rose above their training and circumstance. Drawing on inner strength and moral courage these men overcame the expectations set before them. Other men were weakened and destroyed by war. A final group of men were opportunists. The thought of such men caused Hazen to shudder. These scoundrels took advantage of chaos for personal benefit. Hazen mused that the war had produced the best and worst of men. Hazen found Custer to be of this last type, and he was appalled.

Hazen remembered testifying against Custer in a military court during the latter's student days at West Point. As an officer, Custer had been found guilty of failing to stop a fight between two cadets. Custer was court-martialed, based in part on Hazen's testimony. Save for the war, Custer would never have made it into the army. The need for officers rescued his career. Perhaps now, years after the court-martial, Custer was intent on paying Hazen back. Worse still, here on the western edge of the country, Hazen had little means to discipline Custer, and, frankly, little means to stop him. Custer clearly had no respect for him and saw this assignment in Indian Territory as being given carte blanche from those in Washington.

Hazen watched the snow swirl outside his window. As he pondered his options a Native woman came trudging toward him. She carried a large basket and her arms strained under the heavy load. Watching her, Hazen could already smell the heavily seasoned meat she brought to his door. Steam escaped from the openings in spite of dishtowels carefully rolled and wrapped around the hot dish in the bottom of the basket. He opened the door.

The woman took a tablecloth, cutlery, plates, and napkins from the top of her basket and placed them in perfect settings around the table. Clearly, she had paid attention during her training. Hazen addressed her. "Thank you for preparing this dish for Black Kettle and his men." The woman lowered her eyes, crossed her arms in front of her, and backed into a darkened corner of the room. There she would wait until the men were finished before clearing the plates.

Once again he peered out the window, anxious to start his deliberations with Black Kettle. Through the storm he saw Black Kettle approach with five of his men. They seemed nothing more than light shadows in the storm until they were almost on his front porch steps. They did not knock; they pushed open the heavy wooden door and came in. Hazen smiled. He had expected no less from Black Kettle.

"Welcome. I've been expecting you." Hazen gestured his respect to Black Kettle and the men who accompanied him. "I have asked a Cheyenne woman to prepare a dish of meat for your men. The Cheyennes and the US Army are enemies. We should eat together before we talk. Full stomachs make hard talking easier."

Black Kettle held up a hand in acknowledgment of Colonel Hazen. "Perhaps you do not know this custom: In Cheyenne camps, the chief's wife must feed anyone who comes to her tipi. The tipi is situated in the middle of the camp. There, even an enemy will find hospitality and safety. Perhaps, my friend, since you are feeding someone who is perceived as an enemy, right here in the middle of your camp, you are turning from a ve'ho'e into a Cheyenne." Black Kettle's eyes lit up with laughter.

"Perhaps I am. There is much to admire in the Cheyennes," Hazen acknowledged. "Here, sit down. Please, eat while the food is still warm."

"After we talk and eat, I wish to smoke a pipe with you," Black Kettle continued.

Hazen respectfully answered, "I'd like that."

After his men dished the meat onto their plates, Black Kettle reached out with his spoon and picked out some morsels, still steaming in the dish. Hazen wondered if Custer ever served himself last. He doubted it.

As he chewed the food Black Kettle carefully addressed Hazen, "There is talk in the tribes that the US Army means to make war on Indians this winter. I am here to remind you that I speak for peace. My people have honored our treaties, including the Medicine Lodge Treaty. I signed that treaty last year. The treaty says we will not make war on whites. The Medicine Lodge Treaty also says that the US Army will not make war on the tribes that signed the treaty. My family and band have kept our promises. My men have not made war on whites. Even after my people were massacred at Sand Creek, we did not raise our guns. My wife, Medicine Woman Later, was shot nine times that day. She survived. I was angry and in my mind I longed for war. I longed to paint my body with war paint and ride out against all whites. Only respect for my rank as a peace chief kept me from taking revenge and killing whites. It was a struggle for me. I say this to emphasize how important peace is. My people want peace with your people."

Hazen shook his head and responded. "I know, Black Kettle, that you and your men have kept your promises. You are an honorable man, a man of your word. I must tell you, though, that in spite of the treaty, there will be war. Already a young officer by the name of Custer is arming his men. He tastes blood. Soon he will march to your camp. You are vulnerable. I urge you to move closer to the other tribes."

Black Kettle looked at Hazen, his face a mixture of resignation and determination. "The other Indians do not want us. Since Sand Creek and Medicine Lodge my band has been cast out. The Dog Soldiers are angry with me. They did not want me to sign the Medicine Lodge Treaty. They do not understand why I don't fight back, especially after Sand Creek. They think I'm a fool. Some see me as a white sympathizer. We cannot move to live with the Dog Soldiers. We are camped downstream and are not speaking with the others this winter." Hazen noticed that Black Kettle left out any reference to feasting. Perhaps, with the large game almost hunted out, the Indians were finding it hard to feed their people.

Black Kettle continued, "You, Colonel Hazen, are Custer's superior. My band has cooperated. Can you not put a stop to this killing? To escape *ve'ho'e* violence we walked many days, from Sand Creek north of the Arkansas River south to Indian Territory. We agreed to leave our traditional hunting grounds. Along Sand Creek, tall grass fed our ponies and the trees grew in great groves. Game was plentiful. Now we live in this new land, where the ground is dry. It is harder to feed our families here. Are you telling me we must move again?"

"I am saying that I cannot control all my officers, especially Custer, any more than the forty-four chiefs of the Cheyennes control the Dog Soldiers."

Black Kettle was surprised to hear Hazen compare Dog Soldiers to officers. "Our Dog Soldiers fought in retaliation. They did not start this war. They will not stand by and watch the slaughter of innocents, the slaughter of their wives and children. My band is not a part of the war. We have not spilled any blood. *Ve'ho'e* spill everyone's blood, that of black slaves, of your brothers in blue, of your brothers in gray. Now you want to spill my blood too. I will raise my white flag. I will pray that it will protect us."

"Your white flag will do you no good here. Chief Black Kettle, I implore you, you must move your people closer to the others." Hazen spoke with urgency, emphasizing every syllable. "Damn the Dog Soldiers. You need protection."

Black Kettle was silent for a long time. His face was heavy with concern. Finally he asked, "Can we not move closer to you? Can you not take us in? If I bring my people to the fort will you make a place for them? Our treaty with your army says we will be safe if we come into the fort."

Now it was Hazen's turn to pause. He closed his eyes and took a long breath before answering. "Would that I could say yes to you, Chief Black Kettle. I cannot do as you ask."

Black Kettle pleaded, "We are but fifty families. My men are good hunters. We will provide for our families and live under your protection. Do you know what I am saying to you? Do you know how hard it is for Indians to move close to forts with fences all around? This we must do if we are to live. It would be difficult. Our children would become used to the ways of whites. Their children would be born inside fences and stockades. My grandchildren might not know the vastness of the prairie, only walls. Inside a fort, they would not know the song of the wind; only through windows would they see the greatness of the sky."

Hazen spoke softly, his voice on the edge of breaking. "I cannot help you. General Sheridan is the great war chief. He makes his camp north of the Arkansas River. You have seen how there is much war to the north. It is his policy to kill all Indians, to wipe out your people. Only out of great respect for you am I talking with you. If I were to disobey my orders, I would be arrested and cast out."

"Then we are brothers, Colonel Hazen, each cast out by our people."

"Chief Black Kettle, I will beg you one more time to move your people closer to the other camps. You will find safety in numbers. I must also urge you to move quickly, move tonight if you can."

Black Kettle conferred with his men before answering. "Colonel Hazen, my men are tired. We had hoped to stay the night here in the fort and go back in the morning. We traveled through a blizzard to get here. Now you say we must turn back and walk through this storm and go home?"

Hazen raised his voice in concern. "I am telling you I have no control over a hot-blooded publicity hound. He is his own kind of Dog Soldier and acts alone. He will sniff you out and track you down. Then he will show no mercy. You must return to your camp tonight and move it closer to the others."

Black Kettle remarked, "You have spoken well. We will leave you and return to our camp. Let me smoke a pipe with you in honor of our friendship."

Black Kettle sat on the floor cross-legged and unwrapped a long pipe. His men joined him, creating a circle. He addressed Colonel Hazen. "Please," he gestured to the space beside him, "you sit next to me, in the place of honor."

Colonel Hazen sat next to the peace chief. He watched him take a small pouch from his bundle. Black Kettle reverently placed a few pinches of tobacco into the pipe. He lit the pipe and then stood, raising the pipe to the four sacred directions as he chanted a prayer song. Black Kettle took a few deep inhalations on the pipe before passing it to Hazen.

Colonel Hazen respectfully handled the pipe. He was honored to be included in this sacred ritual. He took a few deep inhalations before passing the pipe to the next man in the circle. Each man smoked the pipe. When they were finished Black Kettle wrapped the pipe and tobacco in his pouch and secured it to his back.

Black Kettle shook Hazen's hand. "I and my men thank you for the meat. I trust I will see you again."

Hazen responded respectfully, "Godspeed your safe return to your camp. Yes, I will see you again." Even as he spoke these words he knew it was unlikely he would ever again set eyes on Black Kettle, and from the look on Black Kettle's face, he knew his friend was thinking the same thing.

The Native woman emerged from her place where she had been sitting and loaded her basket with the cleared dishes. She moved quietly toward the direction of the kitchen. Her eyes averted and her head bowed, she disappeared into the storm, a silent witness.

Chapter Nine

~~

Washita, 1868

MAGPIE JOINED HER band to watch the men in the dance circle. The hunt was a success and the men were grateful. They danced around a large center fire, their shadows casting long elegant silhouettes on the tipis surrounding the circle. Dancers took turns jumping and yelling in high celebration. Those who had killed the game danced the longest. Magpie noticed Big Hawk dancing in the circle. He stayed in the circle, even as others left. Clearly his contribution to the hunt was considered crucial.

As the sunset and dusk faded to darkness, Magpie heard jingles. Eonah-pah walked purposefully toward the dance circle. He moved like a lynx tracking a rabbit. His body was tense and he radiated a raw, wild energy. With every step he took, the jingles on his moccasins and leggings sounded a rhythmic response to the drums. His face was fierce. He had painted his body blue. Half his face was black, the other half red. White stripes ran down his cheeks. He wore leggings but his chest was bare. A medicine pouch hung around his neck. He carried his pistol in one hand and his arrows in the other. He was dressed for war.

At his side Medicine Woman Later walked quietly and with great dignity, her head held high, as if she challenged anyone to question her or the man she escorted through the quiet crowd. She gestured to the drummers to keep beating and led Eonah-pah into the center of the dance circle. As he came into the circle, the Cheyennes recognized him as Kiowa, a fellow Plainsman. He was not known, but all knew Medicine Woman Later and they stepped aside to let him pass.

Eonah-pah started to dance. The drummers noticed his odd

appearance; the war paint contrasted sharply with what had been a festive occasion. Out of respect for Medicine Woman Later and her status as the peace chief's wife, they played for him. The drums beat louder and louder, aiding Eonah-pah in his war dance. As the drums crested he began his war chant. Some of the women started whispering among themselves. Who was this stranger and why was he readying himself for war? A girl, not much younger than Magpie, pointed at Eonah-pah and started to giggle. Suddenly everyone was laughing at him. Magpie could not stay standing and watching any longer. She stepped into the circle, just in front of the drummers, and began ululating war whoops. She let everyone know she believed Eonah-pah. She believed he was dancing the right dance, the dance the night demanded.

Big Hawk stood opposite Magpie, frowning. He was unhappy to see her singing in support of Eonah-pah. If Big Hawk was angry, his calm steps around the circle toward Magpie did not betray his emotions.

"What are you doing with this stranger?" he whispered to her, momentarily silencing her singing. "We don't know him. Why were you down by the river with him? Do you have anything to say to me?"

Magpie was stunned. Big Hawk's words sounded like an accusation. Did Big Hawk think Magpie was interested in Eonah-pah? "Your aunt and I met Eonah-pah at the Washita. He came out of the trees. He came to warn us. He came to tell us about the *ve'ho'e*. They brought an army."

Big Hawk persisted. "Why give your song to a man you do not know? The People will think he is with you, that you are declaring allegiance to him. Tell me you don't know him."

"I have told you already." Magpie was impatient and her words were stated strongly. "I told you, I saw tracks. The army is here. I do not know this man, but aside from your aunt, he is the only one who believes me. You did not believe me when I told you about the tracks in the snow. You only made fun of me." She stood as straight and as tall as she could and in spite of her small stature, she looked Big Hawk right in the eye. "I'll give you this warning, Big Hawk: you should prepare yourself for battle. Eonah-pah can't fight the enemy by himself. Are you with him? Our band trusts you. If you go with him, others will follow. They will be ready for battle. I know a battle is coming. I saw the tracks."

Big Hawk did not answer Magpie and turned away from her. Magpie shook her head in frustration, but seeing that Eonah-pah was still dancing, she continued her war ululations, aiding Eonah-pah, giving him strength and telling her band she supported his dance.

Big Hawk was not gone for long. When he returned to the circle, he too was wearing war regalia. He had not had time to paint his body, but he had donned his medicine pouch, leather war tunic, and war leggings. Keeping time with Magpie's ululations and the beat of the drums, he placed one foot in front of the other until he was fully back into the circle.

Big Hawk began to dance with Eonah-pah. At first the two men barely paid attention to the other's movements. As they continued to dance, their bodies started to move in the same direction. Eonah-pah looked at Big Hawk, and they began to dance in a type of union, mimicking each other's steps and rhythms, creating a bond, a brotherhood between them. Magpie closed her eyes. She could feel their feet pounding to the beat of the drums. She leaned her head back and forced air from her throat, matching her singing to their movements. She called on the spirits to protect Big Hawk and Eonah-pah. *Protect them as they protect us*, she sang and prayed.

As Magpie sang her song, her kinswomen stood silent. The night sky darkened, but Big Hawk, Eonah-pah, and Magpie showed no signs of stopping. After some grumbling, the others drifted back to their tipis. Not one person joined them. Finally, Big Hawk left the circle and turned to Magpie. "I will need to prepare my body paint and weapons. I hope you are wrong about the tracks but I believe you to be right."

Magpie looked deep into Big Hawk's eyes. She saw he was fearful. She knew they were both thinking about Sand Creek. She also knew that by morning Big Hawk's fear would be gone. The circle magnified the courage and resolve he brought to it. His prayer and preparations would further focus his thoughts, making him ready to calmly face the new day.

Magpie listened as Medicine Woman Later had taught her. She listened to the wind howling around her tipi. Curled up in her heavy buffalo robes, she was warm and cozy, but she knew it was cold outside. Small balls of ice pelted Medicine Woman Later's tipi, pinging against the stretched hides. Through the wind she heard small bells on the ponies' harnesses ringing clearly in the darkness. In her mind, she could see her pony foraging for tree bark and standing with the other ponies, waiting out the storm. She heard a newborn cry in a birthing hut on the edge of the camp. *What a terrible thing,* she thought, *to be born during the starvation time of winter.* She heard a tired horse and his rider wade through the river's knee-deep icy waters and clamber up the embankment. Magpie listened to Black Kettle sigh and tether the horse outside the tipi next to where she lay. Black Kettle bent low as he entered through the door flap of the tipi, joining the elders who had gathered there. Magpie was glad she had gathered wood. The men would be warmed by Medicine Woman Later's stew and Magpie's wood.

In order to hear every word, Magpie listened carefully. Black Kettle was the first to speak. "Since Sand Creek, the frontier prairies have exploded with anger, killing, and those seeking to avenge the deaths of their family members. This will only result in more death. As peace chief I have pledged not to raise my hand or the hands of my people against the *ve'ho'e*. But, like many of you, I have young men in my band who are justifiably angry and who do not trust the *ve'ho'e*. They have made war. There has been much raiding and killing. Now the US Army is responding. Colonel Hazen has asked that we move closer to the other tribes. He says that the army will herd us onto reservation lands and that they will make war on us in order to subdue us and follow their ways. What does this council suggest?" Magpie could hear Medicine Woman Later shifting on her heels outside the tipi.

Medicine Woman Later was not allowed inside during the all-male council. Medicine Woman Later contemplated interrupting the council. No woman had ever spoken in council. Did she dare? The image of Big Hawk dancing a war dance with Eonah-pah fastened in Medicine Woman Later's thoughts. As she thought of the dancing and of Big Hawk preparing for his first battle, she remembered him as a sturdy little boy learning to walk. His chubby fists curled around her hands as she supported his first tentative steps.

Black Kettle watched Big Hawk learning to walk. "To honor my nephew's first year I would like to take part in the earthly renewal and seek a vision in the medicine lodge this summer."

Medicine Woman Later thought for a moment before she responded. She knew Black Kettle's decision meant more work for her. She was proud of her skills and her abilities to provide for others in the tribe. Perhaps this would be a good time to show the elders that she and Black Kettle were worthy of becoming leaders not only of the band but of the tribe as well. Besides, what was a little extra work?

"It is right that we should keep the traditional ways. You should honor your nephew after his first year. Since his birth I have saved grain and goods, which I can trade for giveaway blankets and other gifts. I will prepare a feast and a giveaway for when you finish your dance. It will honor both you and Big Hawk."

Black Kettle had emerged from the medicine lodge a changed man. He no longer cared for war. She too had emerged that year as a woman fully aware of her power. She had become a leader in her own right. Now her nephew was preparing for a hopeless battle. She made her decision and this time she broke all the rules.

Speaking through the tipi door flap she implored the men: "We are not safe. The *ve'ho'e* army has sent men on horseback to fight Indians." Magpie listened to her *nahaa'e* beg Black Kettle to move their small band of families upstream to where other Cheyennes, Kiowas, Apaches, and Arapahos had made winter camp. Medicine Woman Later spoke quietly but urgently, "This young Kiowa, Eonah-pah, Trailing the Enemy, has seen signs of horses and wagons. Magpie was out gathering wood today. She too saw their tracks. They are many. I can hear the cavalry drums in the wind."

One man responded, "We cannot move our tipis now. We are tired. We walked through knee-deep snow. The men cannot move."

Medicine Woman Later addressed Black Kettle. "My husband, we are not safe. Let the women strike the tipis. We can move in less time than it takes to start a fire. Are we crazy and deaf?"

"I believe we are safe. This is a protected location." Black Kettle made his decision. "I have run up the white flag. I have placed my mark on their treaties and kept my promises. They will not attack a peaceful village."

Medicine Woman Later urged Black Kettle, "The *ve'ho'e* do not pay attention to their flags. They have already attacked us when we were under a white flag. My husband, you should remember your own history. Let the women strike the tipis. You are tired. You ride. We will walk."

Black Kettle sighed and looked at his men. They were so tired they could hardly sit up. He answered Medicine Woman Later. "Not everyone has your energy. We trudged through a blizzard bearing bad news. Perhaps if the news had been good, we could move, but right now we are tired. Even the horses are tired. Waiting until morning is the best we can do. You can strike this tipi as soon as the sun rises."

Magpie could tell that Medicine Woman Later was not happy with her husband's words. She clucked twice, sounding a bit like an angry prairie chicken, but she knew when she was defeated. Medicine Woman Later held her tongue.

Chapter Ten

Washita, 1868

A FEW HOURS before daybreak Custer ordered the long line of men and horses to halt. They stopped below the crest of a long ridge. Ross straddled a chestnut mare. After hours of straining through dense and fast-falling snow, the mare seemed relieved to rest. Ross worried that during the night his feet had frozen. He looked down and couldn't see them. A dense, low-lying fog shrouded his lower limbs and hid over a foot of newly fallen snow. For miles he had ridden with his boots dangling off the stirrups, flexing his ankles in an effort to keep the blood circulating through his legs. In order to pass time he rehearsed *Wellington's Victory* in his mind. Each time he reached the end of the piece he shifted his weight, trying to warm his body through his movements. He was only marginally successful. Ross slid off the mare, barely holding back a shout of pain as his feet touched the ground. He moved gingerly for a few paces, wincing with every step. His tired, cold blood responded to his movements as it moved sluggishly through his veins.

Custer announced, "We'll stay here for one or two hours. Men, camp in the snow. Expect to attack shortly before dawn." At these words a current of excitement ran through the men. The attack was imminent. Custer continued, "You, Major Elliott, take your men to the far side of the river. Camp there until just before sunrise. Then prepare yourselves. When you hear the sounds of "Garryowen" you will know to attack. You others, I expect silence. We cannot give away our presence. There will be no talking above a whisper."

During the night the storm had moved on. Now a clear moon's

luminescence revealed a winter landscape heavily blanketed with snow. Stands of tall grass bent over, their arched stems heavily weighted with fringes of ice. The ground was soft with layers of snow. With every step Ross broke through a top layer of ice down to at least a foot of softer snow beneath. There was no protection from the bitter cold. For the second night since leaving Camp Supply the men slept on the ground, camping in the open, exposed to the elements. Ross settled in as best he could, crowding close to the other men and the horses, his only shelter built by huddled human bodies.

The two hours until daybreak seemed an eternity. Ross rose from the cold, wet ground. He had rested but he had not slept. Ross opened his haversack, bolted down two pieces of hardtack, the only provisions he had left, then carefully unwrapped the bugle issued to him by the army. In its reflection Ross noticed a brilliant morning star rising in the east. The star caught Ross's bugle in its rays and the brass gleamed in response. Ross gingerly blew warm air into the instrument, trying to warm it in anticipation of playing the charge.

"Hey, Bugle Boy. Time to feed your horse." A cavalry groomsman portioned out two cups of oats for each horse. Ross tucked the bugle under his arm and reached for his horse. She nickered as she ate her paltry meal in one gulp, her soft muzzle Ross's only comfort in the harsh environment. Ross began to rub her coat with part of a blanket. "Well, girl," he said, "we're soldiering now. Hardtack for me and famine portions for you. Let's hope the supply wagons catch up to us soon or this weather will do us in before the Indians can." It felt good to move. The rubbing brought life into his horse and into his arms.

"Time to mount up. Check your weapons, boys. Band members, get ready to sound the charge." Ross's commanding officer quietly relayed information around the makeshift camp and the men hurried to fall into formation. As a band member Ross rode, though he did not carry a full complement of weapons. His job was to play, to inspire the men to battle.

Custer rode a large black stallion back and forth in front of the brass band. "Good morning, lads. A bright morning star has risen. It is a portent for the battle at hand and symbolizes success. By the end of the day we will have killed the enemy and secured the peace south of the Arkansas River. We will have protected the settlers and kept our women safe from the savages." Custer's words rose to a yell as he addressed the band members. "When you play, play loudly and with all your might. Play so that our men camping on the other side of the river will hear you and know when to charge the village. Play so those red savages hear my battle hymn, my song of triumph. Before they see us, before we top this ridge, your notes will strike fear into their hearts. They will hear you and they will know that today is the day they die." As Custer concluded his speech, he raised his sword in front of the brass players, and the weapon became an extension of his arm, like a conductor's baton. He moved his hand up and down, beating out the time to "Garryowen." Then with a yell, Custer slashed his sword down toward the earth, and the band launched the attack.

Ross struggled to play his instrument and ride his horse at the same time. Though he blew into the bugle, he could feel his lips freezing to the metal. Unencumbered by musical instruments, cavalry soldiers on horseback swarmed from behind him and flowed up over a low-lying ridge. When Ross crested the ridge, his heart sank. There below him lay a peaceful village, a small hamlet with maybe fifty tipis nestled in the valley. A large pole stood at the center of the village and on it, waving and whipping in the wind, were two flags: the flag of the United States with its thirty-seven white stars and just below it a white flag, a symbol of peace.

There were no signs of life. The women had yet to start their day by fanning coals into flames. No children scampered around. Even the dogs were still asleep. On the other side of the river in a thick stand of trees Ross noticed hundreds of Indian ponies taking shelter from the cold. Except for the large number of ponies, this was nowhere near a large-scale encampment. True, he had heard from the scouts that the village was small, but this was tiny. Custer, he realized, was deserving of his reputation. He did not tackle large assignments but went for the easy, the vulnerable, and the contests where the outcome was a foregone conclusion. Ross's bugle suddenly sounded tinny and small. *Only a self-absorbed braggart would require musicians to play on such a cold day*, he thought. He tucked his bugle inside his jacket to try to keep it warm and kept on riding toward the village, wondering why he had enlisted. Why was he involved in such a fruitless and pitiless campaign?

In the valley, Medicine Woman Later lay awake, listening to the nine scars she had carried with her since Sand Creek. Twitches and murmurs deep within her flesh had kept her awake all night. Now she heard what she was waiting to hear. An odd sound came from behind the hills. It sounded like a screech owl or a downed buffalo. Bugles and drums from behind the hills on the other side of the Washita filled the air, drowning out the wind. She screamed an alarm. Black Kettle jumped up from his sleeping pallet, immediately awake. He stepped outside the tipi with his gun. Instead of training his sights on the oncoming cavalry he fired warning shots. Immediately, the camp was awakened and cries of terror filled the air.

Magpie was up in a flash. "We must run. Hold my hand," she shouted in the direction of Cricket's buffalo robes. But Cricket was not there. Magpie looked around the dim light of the tipi, panic rising in her veins. Cricket had disappeared.

Days later when Magpie thought about this time, she did not remember putting on her moccasins or grabbing her bundle. She remembered noticing Cricket's bundle still by the tipi flap, and in an odd moment of foresight she grabbed an extra blanket, wrapping it around both bundles and securing them haphazardly to her back with a piece of rope. She worked fast and hard and in a few scant seconds burst out of Medicine Woman Later's tipi in a full run. She ran wildly, darting between the tipis and windbreaks looking for Cricket. She screamed Cricket's name, but in the melee of men, horses, gunshots, and drums, she knew Cricket could not hear her. Magpie could not even hear her own voice. Despair chased and caught her. Her stomach roiled with anxiety. She had been so brave last night, singing protection for the band. Now that she could not find Cricket, all she could think about were her chances. What were the odds she would outlive this day? How could she survive another massacre? Better to die now, to find Cricket in death, and to take her sister to join her father and mother on the other side. She skirted to the back of the camp and found a lodgepole with a small drift of snow around it. There she quickly dug a larger hole. She knew it was only a matter of time before her small sanctuary was discovered. She sank into the snow and, clutching her stomach, waited for certain death.

Big Hawk, his eyes searching to make sure Magpie was safe, saw her run away from the river to the back of the camp. Why would she run away from the protection of the river? Something in the way she ran, haphazardly and with no clear direction, concerned him. He left his own hastily constructed defenses, a turned-over wagon, and, weapons in hand, ran after her. Childhood games taught him to look around lodgepoles and sure enough there she was, buried with her blankets and bundles. "What are you doing?" he practically screamed at her, his voice rising in panic. "Get up. Get out of here."

Magpie, huddled in the small place between tipi and lodgepole, looked up at Big Hawk. Her face was heavy, her eyes filled with anxiety. All she could manage was "Cricket."

Instantly Big Hawk understood and his voice softened. In spite of the urgency of the situation, he implored her, "I'll find Cricket. She'll be okay. Magpie, Magpie," he shook her gently, "move. Soon we'll be seen." He became frightened when he looked in her eyes and saw that their usual sharp focus was replaced with fear. He tried again. He slowed his words and deepened and soothed his voice. As he stroked her hair and arms he repeated his words. "Magpie. I will find Cricket. She will be okay. You need to save yourself. Leave this grave. If you leave, you will have a chance to live. Stay here and the *ve'ho'e* will find and kill you."

Magpie took a deep breath. Gradually her mind cleared and the panic in her stomach eased. Big Hawk would find Cricket. Cricket was smart. Big Hawk was right. Cricket would be okay. She would be okay. Finally, she stared directly into Big Hawk's eyes. "Find Cricket. Find her safe, like you found us at Sand Creek."

Big Hawk looked around. "There's a clear path now to the tall grass. Go. Run. I'll provide cover." Magpie ran toward the tall grass at the edge of the camp. Once there, Big Hawk watched Magpie disappear into the land, like a rabbit scampering into a burrow. He could not see her, but he knew she was watching and he gestured to her an instruction. "Do not move until I come for you." Magpie ducked under the cover of her dull brown blanket and hid by the whispering Washita. There she watched as soldiers on horseback slaughtered her people and destroyed her village.

Magpie watched the massacre. She saw *ve'ho'e* with beards. They wore indigo-blue uniforms with shiny brass buttons. They had carbines, guns that shot many bullets in a row. She could hear the *pop, pop, pop* of gunfire. Smoke from the guns rose from the valley floor, up and over the hills. Some of the soldiers drew their sabers as they rode through the village. She saw them chase down women and children. Slashed bodies contorted in frozen pools of blood.

In the middle of the camp rode a sharply dressed man. He wore black velvet trimmed in gold. His heavy black boots shone with polish. He had obviously taken great care with his long, thick yellow hair, and it waved and shone under a broad-brimmed white hat. She saw him shouting out orders and commanding his soldiers.

She saw Cheyenne men, spilling out of the tipis, trying to defend the village. Eonah-pah, still in his war paint from the night before and fully armed, stood next to Medicine Woman Later's tipi, his spear thrust into the ground as if he were making a stand. From there he shot arrows as fast as he could into more white men than Magpie could count. At his side stood Cricket. When Magpie saw her, she gasped with relief. She was amazed at Cricket's fortitude. The young girl held Eonah-pah's quiver and handed him arrows; as Eonah-pah shot, his arms moved so fast they were a blur. Cricket stood calmly, as if she had been born for the task.

A mounted soldier saw Eonah-pah and Cricket and raced toward them, saber drawn. But Eonah-pah, faster and battle hardened, grabbed his pistol. Before the soldier could act, Eonah-pah aimed his pistol at the white man's stomach and fired. The man tumbled from his horse to the ground. Eonah-pah lunged for the horse's reins, grabbed the man's saber and carbine, and scooped up Cricket. They rode for the river.

Big Hawk saw what Eonah-pah had in mind and joined him. Together they raced toward the Washita. Just in front of them were women who had fled from the camp with their children. The small group plunged into the swirling icy waters wading knee-deep. Magpie could see that the river's tall banks, high above the water's flow, would provide cover and protect the small group from the white soldiers' guns. The next Indian encampment was just upstream around the far bend. She left her hiding place and, risking death to join her sister, leapt toward the river.

When Magpie jumped into the Washita she almost cried with shock. Above the sounds of breaking ice and rapid-fire shots from the soldiers' carbines she heard Medicine Woman Later's call. She looked back. Why would Medicine Woman Later call out now? She saw her *nahaa'e*'s horse, with Black Kettle and Medicine Woman Later astride it. The horse floundered in the deep snow, unable to carry his heavy load. Medicine Woman Later called and sang to the horse, encouraging the horse to carry them forward. They rode as best as they could for the river. The last image Magpie had of Black Kettle and Medicine Woman Later was of soldiers firing on them from the banks above the Washita. Black Kettle and Medicine Woman Later sank with their horse into its waters.

Eonah-pah rode up alongside Magpie. "Here," he shouted in Kiowa. "Take her with you. I have to get back to the fight. You should be safe now but you won't be for long if you don't keep moving. We will count the dead later." Magpie could not understand all he said, but she didn't need to. Cricket slid off Eonah-pah's horse and into Magpie's arms.

"Don't look back," Magpie said as she carried Cricket, trying to hold her above the water. "We need to keep moving," she urged. As she lunged upstream she squeezed Cricket's body. She squeezed so hard it hurt and Cricket pulled back from her sister, wincing in pain. Magpie's hold on Cricket was broken. Cricket cried with alarm as her body fell through the thin ice and hit the freezing water. The current swept her away from Magpie, downstream, back toward the fighting. Magpie turned and pitched through the water, taking long strong strides toward Cricket, trying to keep her balance in the icy current. Magpie slipped and almost fell but she caught and righted herself. In this part of the river, the current was swift and fast. She carefully balanced herself before moving forward and was able to make some progress moving slowly but steadily toward Cricket.

Cricket lunged and cried as the water carried her away from her sister. As she flailed she saw a rock looming out of the water. It sides were shiny but it had a slightly flat top. It was dry. It was as if the rock was inviting her to climb aboard. Magpie also saw the rock and screamed, "The rock! The rock! Grab the rock!" As the water surged toward the rock, Cricket stopped fighting the water. She let the current carry her toward the rock. She risked being flung against it. She knew with complete certainty she had only one chance to save herself. As the water swirled around the rock, Cricket reached out and grabbed onto its flat surface. She felt the water wash over her head. She started to sink into the water, her hands clinging to the rock. In that moment she found a sliver of a ledge hidden under the water. She leveraged her toe against the ledge, leaned into the rock, and with all her might heaved herself out of the water. Once there she clung to the top of the rock, the current spinning around her. She looked like a drowned mouse, exhausted and wet, but felt something new. Her fear was replaced with stubborn determination.

Magpie flung the bundles over her shoulder. She strode toward her little sister, her legs working against the water, full of strength and resolve. When she reached Cricket she hugged her. "Move to the top of the bundles and hang on. I'll need my arms for balance and my hands in case I fall." Cricket climbed over Magpie's head and clung to her shoulders, holding herself as rigid as she could, sitting on top of the bundles. Carrying her sister and the bundles on her back, Magpie cautiously moved away from the current into shallower waters and toward the shore. She carefully placed one foot in front of the other, making sure she had balance and a sure footing before transferring her weight for another step forward.

Once they reached a calmer pool she shifted Cricket to the front of her body and carried Cricket like the small child she was, holding her close, belly-to-belly, trying to keep her warm. When they reached the shore Magpie glanced around. No soldiers were in sight. She listened but heard nothing. They were alone. She put Cricket down and untied one of the bundles. "Here, let's get the blood moving in your veins again," she soothed. She vigorously rubbed Cricket with one of her blankets in an effort to keep the cold from soaking into her little sister's bones. It was then that she noticed the blanket she had grabbed was the same one Big Hawk had worn to court her. It must have been on the top of the pile kept near the door. "This will not do. The colors are too vivid. We'll be found out." Placing it aside she picked up another blanket and continued to massage Cricket's back, torso, shoulders, and limbs, encouraging the blood to flow through her veins.

At first Cricket stood quietly, not making much sound, but as Magpie kept working her over with the blanket, she looked at her older sister full in the face, the realization of what had just happened setting in, and she broke down with a shiver and a cry. "I'm sorry, Magpie. I couldn't keep up. The water was too cold and fast."

"Hush, hush, Cricket. You're okay now. It's been a tough winter already and you haven't had enough to eat. No wonder your strength is gone. Let's just try to keep warm. Here, take my hand. I don't think we should move now. I don't know where the soldiers are. It's best to hide. We'll stay under this blanket. The heat from our bodies will warm us." She looked upstream and saw that other women and children had long disappeared behind a bend in the river.

The girls scrambled up the riverbank and walked partway up a small ridge to a large stand of small trees with thick tall grass. She thought with some irony, *Here we are again, once more hiding in tall grass*. Magpie took off Cricket's wet garments and shook out the colorful blanket. She wrapped Cricket up tight, as tight as a newborn baby. She vigorously rubbed Cricket, desperately trying to warm her sister. The bitter cold seemed to have sunk into Cricket's very bones. Magpie covered herself and her sister with the old brown blanket from her bundle. Completely camouflaged, the girls disappeared into the tall grass.

Chapter Eleven

~

Washita, 1868

EONAH-PAH AND BIG HAWK positioned themselves between the women and children and the soldiers. Firing as fast as they could, they protected the small group from the soldiers until they reached the next Indian camp. There the women and children who had waded for their lives through the waters of the Washita were taken into tipis, stripped of their wet clothing, rolled into blankets and buffalo robes, and placed near warm fires. Cheyenne and Arapaho men, fierce Dog Soldiers who were trained to protect their villages, emerged silently from the trees bordering the Washita on either side. Big Hawk and Eonah-pah looked at each other and exhaled with relief. Big Hawk signed first, "I have to find Magpie and Cricket. I have to make sure they are safe. Talk to my brothers, Eonah-pah. You, Trailing the Enemy, you know strategy. Plan a strategy to save this village. I'll rejoin you as soon as I know my family is safe."

Big Hawk started calling out for Cricket and Magpie, hopeful that they were in a cozy tipi heated by a warm fire and fed hot soup. In tipi after tipi he poked his head through the door flap asking, "Have you seen Magpie? Have you seen Cricket? Where are Magpie and Cricket?" In each tipi the women silently looked at him, deep concern in their eyes, and shook their heads. Finally, in a large tipi crowded with mothers and children, a young boy spoke up. "The last I saw them, Magpie was helping Cricket out of the water. They went toward the ridge."

Big Hawk looked sharply at the boy. "Where?" he asked.

"Just before the big bend in the river where the ridge comes down to meet the Washita. That's where I saw them."

Big Hawk was both relieved and horrified. He was relieved that the last time they were seen they were still alive. He was horrified that they had left the protection of the water. The two girls were on the ridge's slope. They were still out there. He would have to go back for them.

Big Hawk raced back to where Eonah-pah was signing with a group of Cheyennes and Arapahos. As he joined the circle he shook his head.

"Magpie and Cricket aren't here. I have to find them, whatever their condition. I need to know what happened."

Eonah-pah noted his newfound friend's anxiety and responded calmly, signing, "The best way for you to help them is to kill the *ve'ho'e* soldiers. Magpie is a smart one. She'll find cover and hide. After we make it safe for her to come out again, then you can find her." Big Hawk recognized the wisdom in Eonah-pah's strategy. It was better for him to stay disciplined and to fight with a group of warriors. Running through the woods alone was asking for an ambush.

Eonah-pah signaled to the warriors, "It was a small group of soldiers we held off. They wasted many bullets. They were loud. We can surprise them. I say we traverse the ridge and stick to the trees for cover."

Big Hawk, Eonah-pah, and the Cheyenne and Arapaho warriors walked quietly to the trees and disappeared. Each warrior stepped carefully, paused, and listened as he advanced. As they walked they spread out. Each man made sure he could see two other warriors, one on either side of him. It didn't take long to hear the group of soldiers. They had gathered in a small clearing partway up the ridge and were laughing loudly. They clearly had no concern about being discovered or fired upon. They were in the open, no possible defensive position available to them.

Eonah-pah motioned to Big Hawk who relayed the motion down the line. The warriors took protective positions behind tree stumps and trunks and instantly blended into the forest's edge. The few Cheyenne and Arapaho warriors were outnumbered, but they had a clear shot at the soldiers. Big Hawk raised his gun and fired. The shot seemed to come from nowhere. One soldier went down. All of a sudden the soldiers were quiet, tense, waiting for the next shot. They realized their mistake and knelt in the grass. It was only one shot. Perhaps it was just one person firing on them. Eonah-pah stepped away from his hidden position. He was in the open but had a clear shot. He notched his arrow, raised it, and pulled the buffalo-gut bowstring tight. Then he let the arrow fly before ducking back behind the tree. The arrow sang toward its mark. Another soldier went down. At this point mayhem ensued.

The soldiers, now facing battled-hardened warriors, quickly fell back and ran for cover. They ran in the only direction they could—up the small ridge. The soldiers chose poorly, for at the top of the ridge there was no tall grass, no coverage, and no way to hide from the enraged warriors. The surrounded soldiers huddled in a circle and, terrified, fired their guns into the air in a desperate bid for help.

⌒⌒

Just downslope on the side of the ridge that dipped into the Washita, Magpie and Cricket huddled together. Cricket's shivering had lightened but she still shook intermittently. Magpie held her tiny, rail-thin sister close. Under the layers of blankets, Magpie whispered to Cricket, "Did you hear that? Those are *ve'ho'e's* guns. Listen to how often the *pop pop* repeats. They are not firing single shots. They are frightened. That's not the *pop pop* of strategic firing. That's the sound of all-out panic. They are running. Eonah-pah and Big Hawk are winning. Stay still. This may be over very soon."

⌒⌒

Just on the other side of the high ridge Custer heard the gunfire. Had something gone wrong? He looked around and saw nothing. He could not see over the ridge. But he did not bother to climb the ridge. *Surely my boys are doing their job and doing it well*, he thought. He felt confident his soldiers could handle any resistance brought by a group of ragtag savages.

⌒⌒

Eonah-pah silently gestured to Big Hawk and the group of warriors, "They are firing their guns for help. We have them now. Let's finish this." The warriors came out from behind their cover. Staying just out of gunshot range they war whooped battle songs. They circled the terrified men,

83

coming closer up the ridge and brandishing their weapons before falling back. The men on the ridge alternatively fired panicked shots at the Cheyennes and Arapahos, then, desperately trying to summon help, fired into the air. Crazy with fear they fired into the sky, emptying rounds and rounds of ammunition.

The Cheyennes continued to circle and draw fire from the soldiers. One by one Custer's men ran out of bullets. Eonah-pah and Big Hawk could hear that the soldiers were low on ammunition. Eonah-pah unleashed his arrows, his aim lethal. Others joined them. Shot after single shot they killed every man. Berserk with battle rage, the warriors took out their full fury on the dead bodies, desecrating and scalping the soldiers. Big Hawk finally had his revenge. These evil men would pay for Sand Creek. They would pay for Washita. They would not find peace in the afterlife. They would be scarred forever by the wrongs they had committed. As their ghosts wandered they would be marked for all eternity as evildoers, enemies, cowards, and killers of women and children.

Custer heard the guns go quiet and frowned. Should he have ordered a charge toward the ridge? Perhaps it was time to move upstream. Perhaps these savages had put up an unexpected defense. He climbed the ridge and what he saw made him wince in fear. Now atop the ridge, Custer could see hundreds of warriors, Kiowa, Plains Apache, and Southern Cheyenne, advancing along the Washita, ready to engage in battle with the cavalry. He saw contingents of Dog Soldiers riding toward them, guns at the ready. Where the hell did all these savages come from? Clearly, they too had heard the sounds of war. Only then did Custer realize he was outnumbered. Unless he retreated, all his men would perish.

Custer made a strategic decision. He would fake an advance. He yelped to his soldiers, "This is a real battle now. Fire away. Fire into the forest." The Dog Soldiers who had been advancing toward Custer faced a barrage of gunfire and fell back to protect the women and children in the villages. The Indians fanned out, took cover, fired back strategically, and killed a few soldiers who stayed in formation and were unprotected. When the Dog Soldiers fell back Custer ordered a retreat. "Fall back, retreat. Retreat!" His soldiers were all too happy to retreat, and they drove their horses toward the center of Black Kettle's now-abandoned camp.

Surrounded by dead bodies, Big Hawk watched the battle and saw where it was headed. Now it was time to search for Magpie and Cricket. "Please," he prayed. "Please let me find them alive one more time. Magpie is resourceful," he comforted himself. "She will know what to do."

As he started in the direction of the river, Eonah-pah ran to his side. "Go find your family," he signed to Big Hawk. "I'm headed back with the warriors to protect the villages. I will see you there—with Magpie and Cricket."

Big Hawk left the knoll and ran down the ridge back to the bottomlands of the Washita. He hoped to find footprints, side by side, one set smaller than the other, leading away from the river. When Big Hawk reached the river he stopped and sighed with frustration. At the river, along its sides and up its muddy banks, were footprints, many of them of women and children who had fled into the stream earlier in the day. Intermingled in the muddy slosh were prints of horse hooves and boots. At first he despaired of tracking Magpie. Then he thought, *I've always found Magpie. She can hide wherever she wants, but I have always found her. I'll find her this time, too.*

Chapter Twelve

Washita, 1868

AFTER CUSTER ORDERED the retreat the guns quieted and all was silent for a few moments. It was as if the very earth was in shock. Magpie listened to the wind and felt it blow toward the Washita and the Indian camp. In that quelling moment she called out, like a magpie. Downwind hidden in the trees Big Hawk recognized her voice and followed the sound. He realized he had passed right by the girls.

Big Hawk turned. His back to the Washita, he studied the hill. Trees stood in long deep drifts, combing up the flanks of the hill yet never quite reaching the top. It was as if the wind had planted the forest, blowing individual trees into place. The bare outlines of trunks and branches against the snow made it easy to detect movement, but Big Hawk knew how to move through bare trees without attracting attention. For him, the landscape provided cover. Big Hawk could not detect any movement. It seemed as if all the soldiers and their horses had left the area.

The young warrior crouched, kept his body low, and darted from tree to tree. He ran, straightened himself behind tree trunks, paused, listened, and then, staying low, ran again. He was almost to the spot were Magpie and Cricket lay hidden. Magpie cawed again. Big Hawk stood still, listening and straining to see Magpie and Cricket's hiding place. Magpie's caw came from the other side of a small oval clearing. Big Hawk began to feel a small flicker of victory.

It took a while for Big Hawk's eyes to detect differences in the grass, to see the girls. If he hadn't been trained for the hunt, he doubted he would have spotted them. Magpie and Cricket were hidden in a shadow, in a spot where the tall grass grew right up against the trees coming to meet them from the river lands. Even under these grim circumstances Magpie's hiding place drew a chuckle from him. "I should have known she'd choose a shadow," he whispered to himself.

Before moving toward the girls, he stood stock-still, again studying the hillside flanks for any sign of movement, any sign of soldiers on the hill. Then Big Hawk silently moved forward and came out into the open. Once in the open he moved over the snow in the clearing so fast it looked like he skimmed across it. Magpie felt rather than saw his approach. Slight changes in the earth's vibrations whispered of Big Hawk's footsteps. As Big Hawk came near the girls he softly whistled and Magpie, recognizing his signal, emerged from the blanket.

Big Hawk knelt down in the snow. "How is Cricket?" Big Hawk asked, his eyes quickly taking in the girls' condition. Cricket lay still, completely covered. Her breathing was shallow. Her face had taken on a pale, almost blue hue. He was very concerned for Cricket. He didn't know much about medicine but from his experience on the hunt it seemed to him that Cricket's breathing was that of a dying animal. He doubted she had much time left.

"We're cold. Her clothes were wet and I wrapped her as best I could," Magpie said. "The blankets aren't warm enough. We had to leave the river. Cricket hasn't had enough to eat this winter. She has no strength and couldn't fight the current. I can't warm her. Feel her hands."

Big Hawk took Cricket's hands in his. They were ice cold. He stripped off his leather tunic, exposing his bare upper body. "Here, wrap her in my tunic. It should be nice and warm. I've had quite a time warming it this morning." Even though he was alarmed, he deliberately made light of the situation.

Magpie looked at him, gratitude in her eyes. She crawled back under the blanket and wrapped her sister in Big Hawk's leather war shirt. Big Hawk continued to joke: "All those times our mothers made us bathe in icy cold waters are coming in handy now. This is just like taking a bath in the clean air. I'll carry Cricket. You handle the guns." He handed Magpie his weapons. "Be ready to shoot." Her eyes widened. Big Hawk grinned grimly. "Don't worry. Shooting the *ve'ho'e* is easier than shooting rabbits. Rabbits bounce all over the place and know to watch what's coming from behind.

They know how to avoid an attack. These *ve'ho'e* usually stay in formation and they don't move so fast. They also need to listen to their leader before they do anything."

Big Hawk and Magpie walked quietly through the snow toward the riverbank and the Indian camp that lay just up the river. Magpie trained her eyes and ears as she did on a hunt. She was aware her abilities could mean the difference between life and death for the only family she had left.

As they walked toward the river Magpie heard sounds coming from behind them on the hill. Magpie motioned stillness. What she heard made her shake her head in concern. The small party of survivors was still vulnerable. She heard a movement in the brush.

She whispered to Big Hawk, "They are behind us. They will see us."

Big Hawk snorted. "They will not see us. They are the *ve'ho'e*. They won't see us unless we move. They are loud. We know when to be still."

Big Hawk glanced around looking for a protective spot for Cricket. There was a small thicket of brush with very little snow at its center. It looked as if a deer had trampled the grasses, creating a soft space in the harsh wintry landscape. Better to leave Cricket there where she would not be noticed. He squatted and with Cricket still in his arms moved toward the center of the thicket. "Stay still my brave little bug. Don't move. It's just like that game Magpie taught you." Once more and without a word Cricket huddled down into the snow, making herself as small as she could. Magpie and Big Hawk took their positions. They lowered themselves to the ground behind tree trunks. Big Hawk whispered, "Don't fire until I tell you to. We don't want to shoot our guns. That is only a last resort. If we have to fight our way out of here, we will probably die in the attempt."

At first the earth was quiet. The children of Black Kettle's band strained to listen but could not hear a thing. A sudden movement in the trees drew Magpie's attention. Her sharp eyes detected a shiny glint, possibly the barrel of a gun. There in the trees she could just make out a small group of soldiers. She saw the soldier raise his gun but she was faster. As she raised her gun, she caught a glimpse of brass buttons reflecting in the sunlight. She shot instinctively. The button bounced clean off the man's jacket. The barrel of the soldier's gun plummeted to the earth. She thrust the gun back at Big Hawk who handed her his gun and reloaded hers. There in the trees coming straight toward them was a small group of four, possibly five men. Stragglers. Had they lost their way? Magpie wondered why the small group of soldiers had chosen not to follow the tracks of their retreating comrades. The path was clearly marked in the snow. She barely had time to register their movement toward her when Big Hawk fired off an arrow. The arrow sang toward its mark. Another soldier went down. Magpie raised her gun. Her sharp eyes found yet another soldier. This one was even brasher than the first two. Magpie wondered briefly if he had not learned from watching his companions go down. Then brushing all thoughts aside, she shot. A third soldier went down.

Shots were returned and Magpie dropped to one knee. She trained her gun toward the place in the trees where smoke from gunpowder rose. Magpie shot, but distracted, she missed her mark because from the corner of her eye she saw Cricket in Big Hawk's tunic. Cricket had emerged from her hiding place. Big Hawk and Magpie both noticed Cricket standing in front of the thicket at the same time and moved to cover her. But they were too late. Another shot rang out and Cricket sank into the snow. Blood seeped from a small hole in Cricket's side. Magpie dropped her gun and raced toward Cricket. She cradled her in her arms. "The wound is not that bad my little one. Please hang on. We are almost home." But the light instantly faded in Cricket's eyes, and her small body was already cold. It had suffered too much that day. Cricket had no fight left in her and she died in Magpie's arms. Enraged, Big Hawk fired again and again until the soldier with the gun went down.

On the other side of the clearing a skinny white man raised his arms above his head; an odd brass weapon gleamed in his hands. "Don't shoot. I don't want to fight." Ross raised his bugle into the air and, keeping his hands high above his head, knelt down in the snow. He bent his head in submission. He knew he would be lucky to see another day.

Chapter Thirteen

Washita, 1868

ROSS RAISED HIS head. The first thing he saw was Big Hawk's gun trained on him. Then he saw Magpie. She sat on the ground, her legs crossed, a small body cradled in her arms. Magpie mourned and rocked Cricket, holding her like a baby. Ross's features softened as he looked at Magpie, compassion welling in his eyes. These people were a lot like his people. They were no different from everyone else working on the wharves of wealthy Chestertown. *Black, white, American, English, we all want the same things*, he thought to his surprise. Big Hawk saw his look. Instead of killing him, Big Hawk jutted out his chin and with a jerk of his head motioned for Ross to stand up. Keeping his gun trained on Ross, Big Hawk gestured him to lead them back into the grove.

"Magpie," he said, without taking his eyes off Ross, "we must leave. There is nothing more we can do for Cricket. We will come back and mourn your sister after we are sure there are no more soldiers in the area. It is not safe for us to stay here. There may be more soldiers in the area."

Magpie acquiesced. She moved from her sitting position and took the tunic off Cricket's body.

"Here," she gestured to Big Hawk, "you need this more than she does." She laid Cricket's body in the colorful blanket. Kneeling in the snow, she wrapped it around her sister's small body several times and then carefully rolled the little bundle of body and blanket under the trees, partially camouflaging it and marking the spot in her mind. Surely with those rich, vibrant colors she would find her sister again. She listened to the wind in the trees. She listened to the whispering river and spoke to Cricket. "Here you lie by the Washita. Here you lie in the trees. Mother Earth is all around you. Here you are safe and here you will stay until I come back for you. It's time for you to join our parents, Sage Woman and White Antelope. They are waiting for you. I will see you in a land where the grass waves in the wind, where buffalo herds are great. There you will have enough to eat. There you will run free. You will not need to wear your moccasins at night and you will not know fear."

"Magpie, it is not safe. We must leave this place," Big Hawk implored quietly. "I know you need to free your sister's spirit. We can come back. Right now, we need to get out of here. There could still be some soldiers out here."

She wanted to sing to the four sacred directions and give Cricket's spirit a way to find her way home but she didn't dare. Instead, she stood and walked toward Big Hawk. A shot rang out. Big Hawk flinched and dropped his gun. His shoulder slowly began to seep blood. Instantly, Magpie crouched again, her cheek against the rough grass, her body pressed to the ground. More shots rang out around them. Magpie lunged for Big Hawk's gun. "Run. Get out of here. You'll need cover to escape."

"I won't leave you." Big Hawk was fierce.

"You must. You are injured. What can you do to help me here? Run. If you stay they will kill you. Get out of here. I will hold them off."

"Magpie, if you get caught, do as they say. Cooperate. They might not kill a woman." His desperate whispers were hoarse with urgency.

"I will live. Unless you wish to die today, go."

Big Hawk held his wounded shoulder, trying to stanch the flow of blood. Staying low he melted into the shelter of trees toward the Indian encampments.

Coming out of the forest were the two men of Custer's Seventh Cavalry. Their guns were trained on Magpie.

Ross recognized the men as some of the foulest in the camp. They had not been wanted in Eastern regiments so were sent west. Ross remembered Colonel Hazen's words. *Try to do what you can. Try to spare the innocent.*

Magpie steadied her hands. She trained her sights, drew a breath, and prepared to shoot. Before she could shoot, Ross grabbed her, one strong, rough hand locked around both wrists, the other forced her head back into his chest. He clamped a strong chokehold around her neck and forced her to drop her gun. He grabbed it and yelled, "No need to shoot! I got her. I got myself a squaw."

The two stragglers walked heavily on the ground. *No wonder Indians could hear them long before they saw them*, Magpie thought. She wrinkled her nose. They stank. These *ve'ho'e* were unclean.

"Well, well, Bugle Boy," said the apparent leader in imitation of Custer's lazy drawl, "seems you did all right here. She's mighty pretty. You know what they say about Cheyenne women. They are the virgins of the plains. I bet this one's never been with a man." He started to undo his belt. "Indian squaws rape easy." He laughed lewdly.

"Hold on there," Ross intervened. He stepped back from Magpie and aimed Magpie's gun on the leader. "She is my captive and I say when she is used and when she ain't. Right now, she's mine. You can have her after I'm done." His look turned lewd and he made an obscene gesture at Magpie.

"Aren't you full of surprises. You got yourself a deal, Bugle Boy. Let's get back to camp. Tie her up." He threw a corded rope to the second man.

Again Ross intervened. "I said she's mine. I'll guard her. I'll tie her up." When the man with the rope hesitated, Ross said again, more emphatically, "I'll tie her up."

Ross's experience as a waterman came in handy. The rope was cheaply made, rough and scratchy. He made a great show of tying knots, quickly fastening the rope around Magpie's arms and wrists. Once the rope was knotted he helped her to her feet and guided her to fall in behind the smelly men now heading toward the Horseshoe Hills. As they walked, the smelly men now in front of Ross and Magpie, he reached around her back and gave a gentle tug on the rope, and in that one simple gesture, he loosened the knots that bound her wrists together.

⌇

Magpie, Ross, and the smelly men circumnavigated the hills. They walked back toward what was left of Black Kettle's camp. A huge fire burned in the middle of the camp. Custer strode through the middle of the camp. "Burn everything, boys. Burn everything except those buffalo robes. I want decorated buffalo robes in one pile and plain buffalo robes in the other. Nothing else here is of much value."

Magpie watched the soldiers toss cooking kettles, kitchen tools, and knives. Into the fire went elaborately beaded moccasins, cradleboards, shawls, and blankets. The soldiers rolled large piles of cured leather skins close to the flames, stood them on one end, and tipped them into the fire. Heavy lodgepoles and finally wooden wagons were rolled and heaved into the now-frenzied tongues of red and orange. Away from the flames the stacks of buffalo robes grew into two huge mounds. Magpie recognized Medicine Woman Later's stew ladle lying in the ashes by the edge of the fire. She remembered how just last night Medicine Woman Later had fed the entire village with that ladle.

Ross gestured for Magpie to sit on the ground. He gingerly untied her knots and brought her hands in front of her. Magpie looked at Ross with a mixture of suspicion and confusion. He was touching her but he was gentle. There was no roughness in his voice or his touch. He was making it as easy on her as he could without giving himself away.

Magpie shivered on the cold ground, nothing between her and frozen earth except her leather dress. Ross noticed her shivering and spoke to her even though he knew she could not understand him. "Here, let's move you a bit closer to the fire." Half lifting her, he helped her move toward the warmth of the blaze. Then he walked around to the other side of the fire and took two buffalo robes from one of the huge stacks. Bringing one of the robes back to Magpie he gestured for her to sit on it. He wrapped the other around her shoulders. A couple of the soldiers noticed his kindness. One winked at Ross but they said nothing. Ross whispered to Magpie, "There, there. I hope this is okay. This should be all right. I'll be back. Just stay. I'll try to get you out of here."

Magpie looked directly into his eyes. She did not smile but she did not look away either. Ross took that as a sign of cooperation on her part. He hoped to help her, and in order for him to do that she would need to cooperate. "Stay here," he repeated. Then in a moment of insight he gestured to Magpie to stay where she was. Magpie understood and stayed silent. Somehow she knew he would help free her when the time was right.

⌒⌒

"You there, Bugle Boy," Custer gestured to Ross, "leave her. You finish burning these last few tipis and everything that's still in them. The rest of you," he addressed the other men, "let's go finish off the ponies. Come on, boys. This should be fun." He turned his attention back to Ross. "When I come back I want to see all the tipis gone. When you're finished here join us at the bluffs. We've got a lot of Indian horseflesh to kill." Custer strode to his large black stallion, mounted him, and galloped out of the village toward the sound of carbines popping.

The flames climbed high into the sky, licking and eagerly consuming everything until the only things that spoke of human existence were the trampled circles of grasses where the tipis once stood, two large stacks of buffalo robes, a young man wandering among the lifeless bodies strewn along the ground, and a quiet girl sitting by a raging fire.

Chapter Fourteen

~~~

Washita, 1868

ROSS FOLLOWED THE sounds of carbines being emptied into ponies. He could see turkey vultures and crows making huge, slow rings in the sky. Fear urged him toward the circling birds. Crossing over a small stream, he picked up tracks and followed hundreds of unshod pony hooves. He rounded a bend. Sandwiched between cliff and river, tight against the bluffs, were hundreds of carcasses. Ross saw the bodies, stumbled, and retched. Some of the prone bodies were covered with black feathers. It seemed all the scavengers on the plains had descended on the dead ponies. The birds hissed and cawed at one another, occasionally rising in great black clouds, feathers dropping and covering the bodies like funeral shrouds, before settling down and returning to their grizzly task. A fox skirted the edge of the killing field. At first Ross stayed low, not wanting the others to see his revulsion. He hid in the bushes and watched the gruesome scene unfold before him.

Some soldiers shot the horses as others in the Seventh Cavalry rounded the frightened ponies toward the killing lines. Ross saw Custer bragging in front of his men, aiming and shooting. He raised his gun, turned, and fired. Down went a pony. Custer fired again. Down went the fox. The horses knew what was happening and they circled in panic away from the soldiers. The mass confusion allowed some to escape the soldiers' guns and Ross silently gave thanks for their deliverance.

Ross sat for a long time, watching and witnessing. Finally, knowing he had to obey orders, he moved toward the killing field. It seemed to him that the initial excitement of so much blood had worn down and the men of the

Seventh Cavalry, tired of the killing, focused on their task of deliberately destroying the pony herd as quickly as possible. When the soldiers ran out of bullets, they resorted to slashing throats.

One of the smelly men saw Ross in the bushes and walked up to him, taunting, "What do you think, Bugle Boy? There's an awful lot of horse-flesh here. Come on, Bugle Boy. You're supposed to help kill these ponies. Ain't you got no knife?"

Ross responded, "There's a lot of good horseflesh here. We could use a few good pack animals." The smelly man looked at Ross as if he had gone crazy. "This is why we attack during winter months, right? Indians aren't moving. They need places where they can feed their ponies, with lots of grass and wood for their campfires. This killing don't make no sense. The Seventh could use these ponies," Ross persisted.

"A softy after all," the smelly man replied as he walked away.

Ross could see some of the ponies were wounded but still alive, just on the edge of death. He watched as they struggled to breathe. Small wisps of air escaped from their nostrils and hung in the cold air. Some of the wounded ponies moaned, and when they did they sounded so much like people that he became afraid. He walked around the killing field, taking care to keep away from those doing the butchering. He touched the ponies and caressed their sides, watching them die. He tried to bring comfort to a few of the dying ponies.

After a few long hours the soldiers, exhausted with their second massacre of the day, left the Washita and began the long, hard march back to Fort Cobb.

When Big Hawk walked into the Arapaho camp clutching his bloody shoulder, a group of warriors recognized the young man from their long association with Black Kettle's band. Big Hawk knew many of the warriors from the times when the tribes came together to hunt buffalo. Among them was Eonah-pah, and the two men embraced each other as if they were brothers long separated. A woman who tended a campfire called to the other women and together they quickly staked a tipi for him. One of the women told him, "You Cheyennes are always friends to the Arapahos.

Stay here. Stay here with us as long as you have need. There may be others from your band who could use a place to stay. We will welcome all from your band."

Big Hawk was startled when he heard these words. "Are there no others from Black Kettle's band here?" he asked. "Do you know my uncle, Black Kettle, my aunt, Medicine Woman Later? Have you seen them?"

"We only know that they were last seen falling off their horse into the Washita. We think they are dead. We thought you were dead too."

Another woman said to him, "The others who survived are all women and children. Some fled into the river. They are all here and okay. We know that a few women and children were captured and taken to the ve'ho'e fort.

"Do you know Magpie? Have you seen Magpie? Did she survive?" Big Hawk knew it was unlikely, but he hoped she had somehow killed the soldiers and made it to the camp.

"I know Magpie," the second woman replied. "You mean Black Kettle's orphan daughter, your friend. Isn't that right, Big Hawk? She is not here. Perhaps she was taken by the soldiers."

Big Hawk blanched. His worst fears were confirmed. His uncle and aunt were dead. The young woman he wished to marry had not made it to the camp. She was missing, captured, or worse. He reeled away from the woman, staggering with pain and dismay. He found a dirty, abandoned tipi on the edge of the camp. He entered it and collapsed.

Chapter Fifteen

~~

Camp Supply, 1868

MAGPIE SQUATTED IN the snow and rested her head against the logs of the small cabin. The sun was bright and she closed her eyes, basking in its rays. She felt the heat radiate from the logs and warm her back. She thought about the warmth radiating from the fire in her village two nights ago. It seemed a world away, yet she had known the battle was at hand. Two days ago the wind was fierce and angry. Today, Magpie could hardly feel the wind at all. She tilted her head toward the sun with her eyes shut. The sun reached deep into the back of her eyes. Breathing quietly, Magpie saw colors dance across her eyelids. She thought, *I am still here. I am still here. How can I endure? I am here . . . still. Stillness. It will give me strength. I will endure by being still.* She listened closely. When she concentrated, she could hear the sounds of the battle, the awkward frozen notes of the bugles, the thump of the drums, and the *pop, pop, pop* of carbines. And now she was here, in an enclosed space, behind a fence, captured.

Ross had taken her back to Fort Cobb, along with the other women and children taken prisoner during the massacre. She walked the trail with her head bent low, her eyes searching the ground. She walked in reverse the journey Black Kettle and his men had taken just a few days earlier. Along the trail she looked for evidence of Black Kettle's steps, the path he had taken, but the blizzard had wiped away everything. At Fort Cobb the cavalry rested and then set out for Camp Supply, Custer's home base. Ross had led her there as well, tending to her and keeping her away from the other women and children.

Since the moment when Ross tied her wrists in the grove of trees near the Washita, she had not been untied. The rope was prickly and rough. It's scratchy hairs dug into her skin and even though Ross had loosened it, the rope had, in the past day, irritated her skin, creating blisters and red welts. Some welts were starting to drip blood. She had seen how dogs licked their wounds and how that brought healing. Today, though, there were no dogs left in the camp. She brought her hands up and spat on her wrists, attempting to work her spit into her slowly developing wounds. With her hair a mess, her face dirty, and her clothing filthy she did not look Cheyenne. She looked grimy, scratching and clawing at any chance for life.

Ross approached her. Somehow he was able to see through the dirt and blood to her humanity. "Come now. Here, let me untie you. I am sorry I could not untie you earlier. It was too risky. Others might think I was trying to play favorites or free you." He smiled as he spoke. Ross knew she could not understand him, but he wanted to apologize to her. He worked with the knots until Magpie's wrists were freed. She leaned forward massaging her hands and feeling her skin tingle as the blood flowed back into her fingers. "Are you okay?" When Ross finished untying her, he stepped back a few paces. He was uncertain about what to say next. He wanted to show her he was a friend. He was anxious to let her know that he meant no harm, yet was concerned about her safety in the camp. Some of the women had been taken against their will to the soldiers. He did not want that for Magpie and had kept her tied up for her protection. He thought if she stayed tied other soldiers would think she was already claimed. So far the ruse had worked. He sat down beside her, tentatively took one wrist and began to wash it with clean snow.

Magpie allowed Ross to wash her hands and she once again leaned her head against the warmth of the logs. When she opened her eyes again she noticed a man walking toward them. She blinked. Before her stood Custer, legs spread apart, his hand on the hilt of a sword. He rattled his sword and drew near her. His tone was lascivious. "Watch this, Bugle Boy. I'll teach you how we treat female captives. You need to clean up, girl. I bet you're a real beauty. A lovely prairie rose." He mocked her as he reached down to her. Magpie leapt to her feet. She spat at him, swatted at his hand, and scrambled away. She had heard about Indian women taking up with soldiers. She would have nothing to do with that. She was Cheyenne and would fight to protect not only her honor but also the honor of her tribe.

Ross sprang to her defense, instinctively placing himself between Magpie and Custer. Custer threw his head back and roared with laughter. He laughed at them, the sound rough and rude. "I already got myself one squaw. After I wear her out, I'll come after you. You squaws like what I got. Yes, indeed. You'll see who runs things around here. And you," he addressed Ross, "stay out of my way." Magpie could not understand English but she didn't need to. "What are you doing out here anyway?" Custer demanded. "Take her back inside. Confine her to the jail. She must join the other women." He leaned toward Magpie. "Get cleaned up. Best be ready when I send for you."

At first Ross considered talking to Colonel Hazen about Custer's actions but then thought better of it. Custer was known for his ways with Indian women and so far the army had not put a stop to it. Besides, how would he talk to Colonel Hazen before Custer made good on his threats? No, the only way to help Magpie would be to help her escape.

Late that evening Ross fixed a meager supper of hardtack and salt pork washed down with coffee made with melted snow water. After he finished eating, he quietly made his way to the side of the building where he had taken Magpie a few hours earlier. The soldier on duty grinned as he saw Ross approach. "Coming to get a little squaw comfort, are we?" he sneered.

"Something like that," Ross responded. Let them think what they wanted. By morning Magpie would be long gone, safe from Custer's evil intentions.

He made his way into the room where the women were staying. There was one candle placed on the floor, burning in the middle of the room. It was not enough to warm the women and children or to light the room. In one corner was a filthy pile of excrement. The women were confined with no slop jars to relieve themselves. Grim-faced and tight-lipped, Ross moved quietly around the room. As disgusted as Ross was with the conditions of the room he knew he could not save all the captured Cheyennes. He could only save one. He peered through the dim light until he saw Magpie. She seemed to know what was in store for her, for as she came toward him she took off her army-issue blanket and wrapped it around a small child. Her gesture was so similar to how she wrapped the child at the battle that Ross winced.

Placing his hand under Magpie's arm he guided her out the door. She complied readily, not making a sound. *At least she'll know that not all white men are the enemy,* he thought.

"Hey, no one leaves this building," the soldier on guard ordered tersely.

Ross countered, "Oh sure. I've seen the other men coming and going with women. There's not any privacy in there. I'm taking her back to my tent. Don't worry; I'll bring her back when I'm through with her."

"You're all right. I had you figured for a pansy music boy, but you're all right." The soldier grinned, his teeth stained with tobacco. He spit into the snow, marking his watchman's post with a small brown splotch. Ross led Magpie toward his tent. As soon as they rounded the corner of the building he changed direction and led her toward the stables.

The stable was built into the stockade fence surrounding the camp. In this part of the country where trees were scarce, army builders had opted to incorporate the fence into the back wall of the stable. Ross figured if he could get Magpie out through the narrow window in this wall she could walk to an Indian camp and reunite with her people. The window was in the far corner at the end of a long row of horse stalls. The window was not meant for light, only for ventilation and was small, too small for most grown adults. Magpie was birdlike and little. She might be small enough.

He led her down the long row of stalls. If anyone saw them they might think he was getting ready to take advantage of her. Once in the last stall, Ross dug through the straw until he found what he was looking for. He offered a small bundle to Magpie. It wasn't much. He had put aside what he could from his army-issued rations for two days. A small portion of dried buffalo and hardtack was all he could offer her. He knew she had had very little to eat and that it might be a long time before she ate again. She looked at him and shook her head. He tried again. "I won't hurt you." Finally, on the third try, she gingerly took the small bundle out of his hands.

"Come here. Let's give you a leg up. Over and out you go." He cupped his hands under the window and she stepped onto them. She was light, so light he hardly felt her weight. She threw the bundle out before her, then, twisting and turning, she slithered most of her body through the window. Once her arms were free she grasped the roof of the stable and, leveraging her waist against the roofline, she freed her legs. She bent her knees, pushed off from the stable wall, and, half jumping, half falling, leapt into the darkness. A soft thud in the snow and a quiet tap on the other side of the wall let Ross know she had landed safely. He listened for her footsteps but heard nothing. She was on her way.

Ross heaved a sigh of relief and stepped back a few paces into the hay at the center of the horse stall. He paused in the fragrant hay to take stock of his situation. Only then did he think about his next move. He had been so preoccupied with Magpie's safety that he had neglected to plot his own escape. Surely as soon as she was discovered missing he would be fingered as an accomplice, especially since he had been seen taking her from the confinement area. When he had thought about freeing Magpie, he had had no intention of desertion, but now it seemed like the right thing to do. Could he take the risk? The army killed deserters. He knew he had no choice. *Well, that's it then. My parents will kill me if the army doesn't first. Perhaps the US government will spare the life of a mere musician,* he mused. He returned to his tent, grabbed a saddlebag, a bedroll, his trumpet and violin, and returned to the stable. He saddled up a horse and strapped his instruments to the bedroll. He led the horse out into the night. Surely someone out there in this godforsaken ocean of grass would trade a meal for a tune. He turned south. Perhaps he could find safe harbor somewhere in Mexico and then gradually make his way back to Chestertown, his family, and the sounds of the wind on the water.

Chapter Sixteen

~~~

Arapaho Camp, 1868

WHEN BIG HAWK lifted the door flap to the dirty little tipi on the edge of the camp, he entered a different dimension. He refused to speak. He refused to eat. Eonah-pah, concerned for his friend, but also recognizing that Big Hawk needed this time away from the world, brought Big Hawk water and made sure he stayed warm. Eonah-pah found an extra buffalo robe and kept the fire going in the tipi. Big Hawk was grateful for his friend's ministrations but refused to interact with him. Instead, he drifted in and out of awareness.

Over time Big Hawk's mind seemed to sharpen and clarify. He had strange dreams and visions. He dreamt he, Magpie, Eonah-pah, and the strange, skinny *ve'ho'e* were hunting. In his dream they saw a white she-wolf in the distance. On the she-wolf sat a magpie. The magpie pecked at the wolf's skin, as if sitting on a buffalo and eating the little bugs that infest buffalo fur. To his consternation, Big Hawk watched his vision self raise his bow and begin to shoot at the white she-wolf. One of the arrows came dangerously close to killing the bird. "Stop," he called to his dream self. "Do not kill the bird. Do not kill the magpie. Do not kill the white wolf. The white she-wolf and magpie are your friends." The Big Hawk in his dream did not hear his voice and once again raised his bow. Much to Big Hawk's relief the strange white man knocked the bow and arrow out of his hand. The white man spoke to him in a strange language, like that of a dog, harsh and guttural. Although Big Hawk could not understand the language, he knew the meaning of the white man's words. "Killing the she-wolf will only hurt the magpie," he said.

After this vision Big Hawk uncurled from the buffalo robe, sat up, and warmed himself by the small fire in the middle of his tipi. He saw that his shoulder was cleaned and covered with bandages soaked in witch hazel. Over the witch hazel the medicine woman had sung and layered on clean strips of white cloths that bound his wound together. He had no memory of anyone taking care of him or changing the bandages on his shoulder.

He sat and rocked on his heels for a bit, wondering about his strange vision and also about Magpie. His last image of her was of her being led away by that sickly-looking white man who showed up in his dream, the one with the odd weapon which glinted gold in the sun. He hoped the woman by the campfire was right. He hoped Magpie was alive, even as a prisoner. The smoke rose in a straight line from the top of the tipi where he watched it spiral into the wind. As he watched the smoke rise he thought, *This is what I've come to, kinsman of Black Kettle and Medicine Woman Later. I have no band. My people are dead. I am unknown and living in a small, dirty tipi.* Remembering his family and his aunt's beautiful, large white tipi, the only home he had ever known, he bowed his head in grief.

Eonah-pah sat nearby. He was concerned about Big Hawk but had chosen not to speak to Big Hawk about his brooding silences and fitful dreams until now.

"You are worried about Magpie?" Eonah-pah signed.

Just to have her name mentioned made Big Hawk wince with anxiety. "Yes."

"Big Hawk, hear me. She is resourceful. She will find her way here. I am sure."

Big Hawk was quiet for a few seconds then signed back, "I know she can take care of herself, but I am frightened for her. She is a beautiful young woman. You know how captured women are treated. I failed to take care of her. I failed to protect her. If anything happens to her, it is my fault."

Eonah-pah's hands and fingers moved rapidly. "You were shot. You had to leave. How would your death help her? In times like these it is an honor, it is our duty, to stay alive. Even if only to fight again for one more day. Perhaps you lived so that you can fight again."

Big Hawk shook his head. "I've done a lot of thinking in the past three days, in the time since the attack. I have not purified myself, but I've hardly eaten. My thoughts are strong and clear. I tell you now, I am done with fighting. My uncle, Black Kettle, was right. We can fight forever but we will never win. We will only be killed. Fighting will only bring death. If we keep fighting, eventually we will be attacked again. The only way to survive is to walk Black Kettle's path. The only way to survive is to make peace."

Eonah-pah responded, his gestures becoming stronger and more emphatic. He swore as he signed, "I will never make peace with whites. I will teach my sons and the sons of my sons to fight back, to defend our way of life, to protect our land and our people. My people will fight for our lives. I am surprised to hear you say you will not fight. Your Cheyenne people will not follow you. They will not want to die like dogs. My band, my tribe, the Kiowa, we will stand and fight."

Big Hawk smiled ruefully. "If you do not learn to live with the *ve'ho'e* and learn their ways, you will have no sons."

"Better that than to give in. Better to fight back than to turn your heart away from our ways and toward theirs and to become one of them. It is better to die."

"No, sometimes it is not better to die. Sometimes it is better to survive. To survive is to hope for the future. When you die the future is no more. I will never become a *ve'ho'e*," Big Hawk responded. "I will never be like them. I will always be a Cheyenne, but I will teach my people how to live among them. We must learn to do that if we are to remain."

"I tell you, my brother, we fought together and you are a great and brave warrior, but there are times when I simply don't understand you."

This time Big Hawk's smile broke through his consternation. Eonah-pah was surprised to see Big Hawk smile. It was his first smile in days.

"I will always remember fighting by your side. Your strength, your powerful medicine saved me . . . and many of my people. I will always be grateful. We will speak your name and your deeds will be recounted around Cheyenne campfires for generations to come."

Now it was Eonah-pah's turn to smile. "In spite of our differences, we will always be brothers. You are my brother and Magpie, when she becomes your wife, will be my sister. Perhaps you should break your fast. Let's walk outside and find some food. It's been a few days since you've been out of this tipi."

"Okay, my brother. A walk in cold, wintry wind always makes a Cheyenne feel at home."

The two men laughed as Eonah-pah held open the tipi door flap before following his friend into the camp.

As the men walked through the camp, a young Cheyenne boy ran up to Big Hawk raising his arms, asking to be picked up. Big Hawk almost wept at the gesture. It was the small boy who had told him where Magpie and Cricket were hiding on the ridge. This child had lived through the horrors of war, yet he still wanted to play. His spirit continued to seek happiness. In that simple gesture, Big Hawk understood now that he was no longer a child. Battle and the aftershocks had transformed him into a thoughtful adult, ready to take on the responsibilities of leading and protecting the survivors of his band. With his good arm he tussled the young child, awkwardly flipping him onto his shoulders. Standing beside him, watching all this was Eonah-pah, and after Big Hawk had the child settled on his shoulders, Eonah-pah touched Big Hawk on his arm and pointed.

There was Magpie, with a colorful blanket wrapped around her waist belted with string. Was that his courting blanket? Had she gone back for Cricket's body? Her hair a mess, her face streaked with traces of tears, she walked quietly into the camp. She walked softly but with great determination, as if her feet were moving on their own with no consideration for the rest of her body. Her face and body said she had just journeyed from hell. She was past the limit of all human endurance, existing on stubbornness alone.

The woman who tended the campfire straightened from bending over her cooking to look as Magpie passed. The woman recognized the haunted look in Magpie's eyes and her dogged, exhausted gait. The woman ran after Magpie and brought her to her fire. "Here child. Sit. Warm up. Have some meat. Here, have some skillet bread." Magpie could not speak, though she tried.

"Quiet now, just sit and eat. Drink some hot water and strong coffee."

Magpie knelt on the cleared ground around the fire. She reached for the skillet bread. As she slowly chewed the bread she looked into the small flames and thought about how her life had been shaped by fire. The massive fire built by the soldiers had destroyed everything in her village. There was nothing left from her former life except memories and bad stories. Now fire was bringing healing into her life, warming her body, and feeding her.

Without taking his eyes off Magpie, Big Hawk placed the child on the ground and walked quickly to Magpie's side. Magpie sensed his presence.

She looked up and watched him coming toward her, not taking her eyes off his face. He moved with such fluidity and grace that his footsteps seemed to skim the ground. He walked right up to her and stood looking down at her for a few long seconds. Then he knelt down beside her by the fire. She touched his bandaged shoulder and gently placed her hand on his other arm. He reached out and with a whisper of a touch caressed her hair again and again. He straightened and leaned back from Magpie just enough so that he could run his fingers through her hair. Combing her hair with his fingers, he carefully stroked the tangled mass of long black locks back from her face. He reached toward her waist and untied the blanket. As he shook it out, his thoughts were confirmed. It was indeed his courting blanket, the blanket that Magpie had used to wrap Cricket. Amid the vivid colors were bloodstains, dried and browned but still recognizable as bloodstains.

"Did you find her?"

Magpie looked at him mutely. She took another drink of water and rasped out, "All I found was this blanket. It was in a heap near where we left her. I looked and looked. Her body is gone. Do you think they took her body? Did they burn her body along with everything else?"

"Magpie, I don't know."

"My wrists hurt." She extended her arms toward him.

Big Hawk turned the inside of her wrists out toward him and noticed they were angry, red, and swollen, with pus seeping through open sores.

"Let me help you. Let me take care of you."

He placed the blanket around Magpie's shoulders. She was weak, barely able to stand. He wanted to take her into his arms and carry her to his tipi, but his bandaged shoulder was still painful and prohibited movement. Instead, with his good arm he helped her from the ground and let her lean against the strong side of his body. Slowly they made their way across the village grounds.

Just before Big Hawk and Magpie got to his tipi he became aware of another presence. The woman from the cook fire had followed them. At the door flap she offered up a skillet of meat, steaming from the fire.

"She has lost much strength. She will need all we can give. Aside from her wrists, I hope her body is okay, but if you wish I can come back in a while to check it for bruises or injuries. We need to bathe her and bandage those wrists. With your permission I'll help her." Big Hawk's face was a mixture of concern and gratitude. He balanced Magpie, helping her to stand on her own. She swayed a bit with the effort. Taking the skillet from the woman, he opened the tipi's door flap and beckoned for Magpie to go inside.

Magpie looked at the door flap, hesitating before she stepped into the tipi. This was not much of a wedding. If the massacres had never happened and her parents were still alive, the families would have exchanged gifts. There would have been a giveaway with horses, blankets, saddles, sugar, coffee, fabric, and cooking pots. This stepping into a tipi with no ceremony and no tribal recognition did not suit her. Yet, she knew her home was with Big Hawk. They had already survived so much together. She recalled the last time she had felt Big Hawk's strength leading her into a new place, a new life. Then she had held Cricket, curled up in her arms as Big Hawk had carried them both away from Sand Creek. Magpie shook with recognition. She remembered the blanket. This was Sage Woman's blanket, the one her mother had thrown over her daughter as she lay dying. With Big Hawk's good arm around her, Magpie clutched at the blanket and wept. Then she stepped into the tipi and a new life with Big Hawk.

PART TWO

1968

Chapter Seventeen

Clinton, Oklahoma

LUKE WALKS WITH THE WIND squatted down and eyed the steel fence posts rising toward the horizon in a long straight line. The white posts stood out against the red clay dirt. As they disappeared over a low rise toward the river they drew the eye back into the landscape. *The setting looks like a scene from a Renaissance painting*, he mused, *as if the painter was experimenting with perspective.* Luke enjoyed his freshman classes, especially his art class, but coming home for spring break, getting a breather from his books, and working with his uncle was always a pleasure. Neither man spoke much. They had worked together for so long that they knew each other's ways; they moved around each other like dancers in an elaborately choreographed rendition of barbed wire, hammers, steel pikes, and wood posts.

"We need to reinforce that fourth post. It looks weak. The buffalo will find it quickly, and that's where they'll make their escape," Luke informed his uncle.

At Luke's remarks Two Feathers allowed a small smile. "Your *nahaa'e* let me know that we need to build the strongest fence in the county. It has to be buffalo-proof. She told me she'll round up escaped horses but not buffalo."

Luke perked up immediately. "I agree with my *nahaa'e*. Let's raise horses instead of buffalo. Horses are a lot easier and you can win prize money."

"How many horses and trophies do you need, son? You've already won every riding contest in the state. It's a good thing you're in college. It's time to give the other guys a shot at stardom and glory. No, I'd rather raise buffalo. They belong on these plains. Horses, as you know, came with the Spanish conquistadors. They are not native to us. Besides, I've already ordered the buffalo from a rancher in Texas."

"Auntie won't like it when you leave on speaking tours and the buffalo get out. Maybe Dolores White Calf's boys can help when you're away," Luke offered.

"Dolores's boys would love to round up buffalo, but they won't need to. This fence will hold them."

Luke laughed. "Whatever you say, my *naxane*, but you know as well as I that no fence around here can hold buffalo. They are tricky creatures. If there's a way out, they'll find it."

"Let's do our best. Let's fix that fence, and then it's time to work with a different kind of post."

"You in charge of finding the lodgepole for the Sun Dance again this year?"

"Yes, I have my eye on a tree near the Washita, out near Cheyenne. It's big enough. Those big old ones are getting rarer and rarer. You want to see it?"

"Cottonwood, I hope."

"Yes. It's the best, and some of the strongest wood we have. It's tradition to use a cottonwood lodgepole. Those trees mean a lot to our people."

Luke peered at his uncle. "You sure you want me to go look at trees with you?"

"Yes, I do. There are worse ways to spend a Saturday afternoon. Lots of pretty country out that way too."

Luke smiled. "Can we stop at the little church that serves up burritos in the sanctuary? Is that place still functioning as a restaurant?"

Two Feathers remembered, "When I was a kid, it was full of people, whites and Cheyennes. Now, no one attends services. Sure . . . we can stop there."

"How's the town doing?"

Two Feathers shrugged. "Same as all towns around here. Not very well." Then he grinned. "Not too many people want to drive all that way for a burrito."

"My burritos? I like them sanctified."

"Hmm . . . a little spice on your communion bread?"

"Something like that."

Luke looked at his uncle. Two Feathers was a devout Christian but he also kept to the old ways. He was one of the most traditional Cheyennes around. He taught the Cheyenne language to youngsters in the local school and told them stories about their Indian heritage. He was one of the main organizers of the Sun Dance every year. He was also a minister in a local church. Luke always wondered how Two Feathers could stand, one foot in each world, red and white, Cheyenne and Christian, without falling over. It was a balance Two Feathers had maintained his entire adult life.

Luke remembered when he was nine years old asking his uncle about the circle and the cross. Two Feathers had responded, "You know the sacred medicine wheel?"

"Of course."

"What does it look like?" Two Feathers had asked.

"It's a circle."

"What about it? Is there anything different about this circle? What do you see in the circle?" Two Feathers had turned toward his nephew.

"It's a circle divided into four."

"Yes. Quadrants."

"Quadrants." Luke practiced the new word.

"What colors does the medicine wheel have in it?"

"Each quadrant has a different color. White, red, yellow, and black."

"What do you know about these colors?"

Luke had heard Two Feathers talk about the sacred medicine wheel and its colors all his life.

"White is my favorite. It's the color of dawn, the color that represents when the spirit world is closest to us and can speak to us."

"That's a good interpretation," his naxane *had teased him. "It sounds kind of familiar. The colors are separate, yet they all work together. They have different meanings, yet all point to understandings. They are central to Native American spirituality."*

"The circle symbolizes the concept of the Cheyenne Life Road. To the northeast, the color white represents small plants or children. To the southeast, the color red represents willows or young men and women. To the southwest, the color yellow represents the cottonwoods or mature men and

women, and, finally, to the northwest the color black represents cottonwood branches or elders. The circle also represents the seasons and renewal. It is never-ending."

"What about Christianity?"

"What about it?"

"I don't believe in it," Luke challenged his naxane.

Two Feathers smiled at Luke. "I will never tell you what you must believe. That is something you need to decide for yourself. Only after you seek the truth will it come to you." Then he asked, "What is the most important symbol to Christians?"

"Jesus on the cross."

"What does the cross mean?"

"It means Jesus suffered and died for us, for our sins."

"Did Jesus stay dead?"

"No. Christians celebrate Easter, when Jesus rose on the third day."

"What do you think this means? Why is this story so powerful?" he asked rhetorically. "Some people believe Jesus actually rose from the dead. Others prefer to believe in the powerful imagery and symbolism of the story. The cross stands for ultimate forgiveness. It stands for redemptive suffering. The whole world and everything in it is redeemed. The cross makes the statement that love is the most powerful force on Earth, able to overcome suffering and to transform human brokenness into wholeness."

"I don't believe God wants us to suffer. As Indians we've suffered long enough," Luke retorted.

"Yes. You have your own beliefs and perhaps that's where you and I differ. As a Christian I carry the cross. As an Indian I live in a circle, inside the medicine wheel."

Perhaps the spicy communion comment was appropriate, Luke mused. Over the years Luke had often thought about that conversation and the rich symbolism in his uncle's statement. What was it like to carry the cross and live in the circle? How had his *naxane* done it? Was that to be his path as well? He had never been baptized, and at this age he had no inclination to do so. Yet Luke was in college. He had never lived on a reservation. In fact, he had lived outside the Indian community more than he had lived in it. He had one foot in the white man's world and one in his own, also straddling the differences as his uncle had before him. He did not make the same choices, and yet, in some ways, the decisions he was faced with looked much like those of his uncle at his age. The same choices seemed to circle through the generations, from elder to child, different in degree but not in kind.

The two men worked hard for another two hours, digging holes and placing posts in the ground. Finally, Two Feathers straightened up and, without saying a word, walked to his pickup. He opened the door of the truck and leaned against it, folding his arms over the rolled-down window, one leg resting on the step bar. His wife had placed a warm thermos of coffee on the front seat. He poured a cup of the bitter brew. He liked it Indian style, no cream or sugar but as black and strong as she could make it. The sun-warmed steel of the truck felt good against the new blisters in his palms, painful reminders that he didn't work with his hands much. He rested and watched his nephew.

Luke kept working. He strained himself, putting his back and shoulders into the work. He did not swear or make exclamations as he wrestled the fence posts into resistant ground. It seemed the red earth of Oklahoma wanted to spit back the poles over Luke's head and into the air. When each post was in place, Luke eyed it and then worked with a level to make sure it was in straight. Every so often he gave the posts a hard strategic kick and they fell into line.

Two Feathers waited for Luke to tire, but he kept on going. First one, then another, then a third post fell into place. After a half hour Luke was still working away. The more he watched Luke work, the more Two Feathers realized that he was aging. *I used to work like that*, he thought. Finally, Two Feathers called to Luke, "I'm done with hard labor for the moment."

Luke straightened from his task. "Seems like you've been done with hard labor for a while now."

"Humph." Two Feathers allowed a small smile. "Let's go toward the Washita and look for that lodgepole."

"What? That's not hard labor? Who is going to cut down that tree, haul it, strip it, and plane it? Sounds like hard labor to me."

"We're just looking today. I won't bring my tools, promise."

"Okay," said Luke, giving a final fence post one last kick. "Let's go. It's sanctified burritos on the menu today."

Chapter Eighteen

~~~

Cheyenne, Oklahoma

THE ROAD UNSPOOLED through western Oklahoma like a thick black ribbon up and over the hills. Luke and Two Feathers rolled down the pickup windows to smell the freshness of early spring and to enjoy the sun's warm rays on their skin. The wet, red fields had carved the gently rolling earth into sharply defined squares and rectangles. Green shoots planted in long, straight rows stretched back from the road. As they drove, Two Feathers noticed how the landscape was softened by curving lime-green billows, the tops of trees peeking over the tall embankments of small stream-fed arroyos. On a quest for scarce water on the semi-arid plains, the trees grew along the streambeds, following the waters' sculpturing flows. Two Feathers frowned slightly. None of these trees was big enough for their needs. All the trees along the streambeds were thin trunked, not strong enough to be a lodgepole at a Sun Dance.

"How do you know which tree to pick for the Sun Dance?" Luke asked.

"I talk to them," Two Feathers answered. "I ask them if they're ready to be part of the ritual and if they have the strength for renewal. Renewal takes strength. People who seek renewal find it in many places, sweats, dances, songs, even the tree we use for the lodgepole."

"Okay, I agree, renewal takes strength. That makes sense to me. But talking to trees?" Luke was skeptical.

"When your great-great-grandmother was a girl, it is said she used to go to Sand Creek and talk to the magpies in the cottonwood trees. After the massacre there the tribe moved south."

"Did she talk to the birds after the massacre?"

"I don't know. Probably. In our family, we have a long history of talking to God's creation."

Luke winced. He did not like to hear his *naxane* place his family's history within the context of Christian language. Instead of arguing he said, "You've told me many stories about Magpie and her family."

"Her family is your family. Her people are our people. The People. The Tsitsistas. Their past is not that long ago, only one hundred years. Some people live that long. Medicine Woman Later talked to cottonwood trees. She listened to them whisper and learned many things."

Luke knew enough not to be openly critical of his uncle. Still, again he felt uncomfortable. His uncle was a college-educated man, and here he was talking about tree whisperers. Lately, it seemed that at every turn Luke was at odds with the man who had raised him.

Two Feathers did not notice Luke's discomfort. "This talking about Medicine Woman Later and Magpie puts me in mind to stop at the museum in Cheyenne. How long has it been since you've been there?"

"Years. I guess you want to see that display of Indian bones. Is she still there?"

"Yes she is," Two Feathers responded. "Even though the townsfolk there know how we feel about displaying the bones of our people, she is still there. Such insensitivity is hard to believe. And these are not just any Indian bones," he added. "We know these bones were collected by the army after the Washita Massacre. We know that this was a massacre victim. We even know where her bones were found. The army kept records." Two Feathers recited, "Box 166, Bones of Girl, approximate age: six, found in tall grass, south side of Washita battle site."

Luke had no words. He just sat and shook his head.

Two Feathers and Luke arrived in Cheyenne. They drove down the dusty main street. It was one of those towns typical to the Great Plains. Luke remembered standing as a child in the middle of the road at one end and looking straight down Main Street to where it became flat prairie. Small, squat buildings were embraced by an overpowering sky. Halfway through town sat a small dark building. The words BLACK KETTLE MUSEUM were prominently painted on its side in large white letters. They got out of the pickup, crossed the small gravel parking lot, and, as they walked into the building, turned on the lights.

There she lay, nestled among the exhibits about the Southern Cheyenne tribe and the explanations of the massacre that had happened one hundred years ago. Her bones were arranged carefully in a glass display case. The body was slightly tilted so that the bullet's path could be seen. The bullet had shattered her left rib as it rammed into her body. Two Feathers stopped. He placed his hands on either side of the case, as if he was ready to talk to the bones. He did not speak. His face contorted in visible grief. Luke saw his uncle's face and quietly made his way to another part of the exhibit.

Two Feathers prayed over the bones. "Father Spirit who protects families, Mother Spirit who loves and nurtures children, You, who are many and one, bless this little child. This is a child of our family. Her bones are on display and she is not at peace. She is not at rest. Her soul still wanders the earth. Protect her. Help me to find a way to bury her bones so that they might decay and send her soul home to her people. Help me find a way to bring peace to this little girl."

A small white man in a standard-issue white-collared shirt and dark pants approached Luke. "Tell Two Feathers when he's done praying over those old bones to come to my office. I have a proposal for him."

Not wanting to interrupt his uncle, Luke said, "We're here to find a lodgepole for the Sun Dance and don't have much time. Can't you call him later?"

"I've been waiting to talk to your uncle face-to-face for some time now and it's getting urgent," he responded. "You know this is the one hundredth anniversary of the Battle of the Washita."

Luke blanched. *He means to say "massacre,"* he thought, but he held his comment and instead said, "My tribe is aware this is a commemorative year." His blank face hid his emotions, as he had been taught since childhood.

The director sensed something was not right. Even though Luke kept an even composure, his face had lost its animation. It was like talking to a mask. The director pretended ignorance and plowed through his agenda. "Some of us have been talking about how best to remember the battle. We've come up with a plan and we'd like to run it past you, see what you think. It would be a kind of celebration." This time, against his will, Luke visibly reacted and stared at the museum director in shock.

"You'll need to talk to my uncle. He's the peace chief and the one in our tribe who is responsible for these kinds of decisions." Luke struggled to get his words to flow evenly.

"Can you send him to my office when he's done?" The director cocked his head at Two Feathers's figure, praying and leaning over the bones of the little girl. Luke looked at the museum director in dismay. He couldn't imagine how Two Feathers would take the news.

Chapter Nineteen

Cheyenne, Oklahoma

AS LUKE APPROACHED him, Two Feathers finished praying. "You're wanted in the director's office." Two Feathers looked at Luke, a quizzical expression on his face. "I'll let him tell you what he wants," Luke said, a note of warning in his voice.

Two Feathers did not need to ask Luke what his tone meant. He knew he was about to be ambushed by the museum director.

Two Feathers slowly made his way past the small-town exhibits, the glass cases with artifacts that hadn't been dusted in years, the stuffed animals and owls meant to educate school children about the wildlife that used to inhabit the area, the small, grainy black-and-white photographs of farmers standing in front of dugout cabins, the women and children thin and looking at the camera with questioning eyes. He entered the director's office and sat down heavily on the hard oak chair the museum director offered his guests.

The director got right to the point. "As you know, the town of Cheyenne is facing hard times. We would like to attract tourists, put this place on the map. Everyone knows about Sand Creek, everyone knows about the Battle of the Little Bighorn. There are scores of Indian sites that attract tourists and tourists have money to spend. Money this town could use. No one knows about Washita. No one knows about the history here."

He paused. Something in the back of his mind was alerting him. A small voice tried to speak to him, tried to let him know that based on Luke's reaction, perhaps this wasn't such a good idea after all. He sensed quite vaguely that his next words might be deemed offensive. In that moment he pushed the voice away and made a decision for the town over the tribe.

"We would like to do a reenactment of the battle. We need your tribe. Your tribe could lend us a hand, set up some tipis on the bottomlands near the river, and participate in this historic event. We could advertise 'The Reenactment of the Washita Battle' throughout Oklahoma." His voice rose in excitement as he spoke. "Folks who are interested in Native American history and the famous Seventh Cavalry would pay for tickets to come see the reenactment. The Washita Battle would no longer be an overlooked footnote of history. And, as you know," he repeated, "this town could use the money."

Two Feathers could not believe what he was hearing. Would his tribe be willing to reenact that awful event in their history? He hesitated and then responded, "That massacre resulted in the deaths of my great-uncle, Black Kettle, after whom this museum is named. My great-aunt, Medicine Woman Later, died at the Washita, as did most of my family. Only a few survived. I don't see how helping you is a possibility. You ask too much of me . . . of us."

The director persisted. "Two Feathers, we could really use your help. This town is dying. For Chrissake, the church is selling burritos. You know how bad it is. If we could get tourists here, attract some money, we might be able to turn it around. This kind of thing would benefit your tribe as well."

"How would participating in a reenactment of a horrible massacre benefit my tribe?"

"It would educate people about the historical event."

"You mean it would teach tourists about a brutal massacre, an attack on a peaceful, sleeping Indian village?"

"Yes, I suppose so. Didn't Black Kettle fight back?"

Two Feathers was at the end of his patience. He reprimanded the director. "You don't know your history very well. Black Kettle had just gone to Fort Cobb to plead for protection. He was turned away. Just one year earlier Black Kettle had signed the Medicine Lodge Treaty, saying that he would not allow the men in his band to make war on whites. He stuck to his pledge. Much good it did him." After his short speech Two Feathers sat very still for a long time. His face was now completely impassive. His lips were pulled together until all that could be detected was a slightly crooked, compressed narrow line. Finally he said, "Give me some time. I need to think about it."

Two Feathers's answer was not what the museum director had hoped for. The museum director held in a quick retort. He wanted to say, *No problem, you think about it while this town dies.* Instead of responding negatively, he said, "You do that. You think about it. You're a good man, Two Feathers. Hey, how long have you been peace chief?"

"Only five years. I have much to learn."

After walking Two Feathers to the door, the director slapped him on the back. "Hey, it's always good to see you. You're not like the rest. You're easy to talk to." With that remark, he shut the door and retreated into his office.

Two Feathers and Luke left the museum. In silence they drove along a fragrant prairie field to the massacre site. Both men got out of the car and walked down the long slope that led to the Washita. They walked through the grasslands, the stems red and green with new growth waving in the unceasing wind. They walked through the bottomlands to the river's edge. The sun glared hot and high in the sky.

Two Feathers left Luke by the river and diverged from the path. He walked through the tall grass, his footsteps swishing through the reeds, chasing up grasshoppers and butterflies. He felt the intense Oklahoma sun on his face as the wind whistled around his ears. Sometimes the never-ending wind reminded Two Feathers of stories about Medicine Woman Later. Here she was, still blowing, still full of energy, still warning her band to flee.

Could Two Feathers, his band, and other Cheyennes pretend to be attacked? Could they pretend to die, just as their ancestors had died a hundred years ago? He sang to the four directions and then sat down under a cottonwood tree growing by the riverside.

"Father God, Mother Spirit," he prayed, "what is your will? What should I do? Show me the path I should choose." The image of the little girl's bones in the museum stayed with him. He looked at the river and saw his own children in his mind. He saw grandchildren not yet born, playing and splashing in the Washita, creating swirls around the roots of the cotton-wood trees.

He could not make a decision based on how he felt. He needed to make a decision that was good for the tribe, good for seven generations. He would take the question to the elders. Again, he sang to the four directions, and his song floated high into the sky. He took long, deep breaths. His mind was finally at peace. He turned and walked, his footsteps taking him away from the river.

"What did you decide?" Luke had followed Two Feathers to the cotton-wood tree, but he had paused at a respectful distance.

"That cottonwood right there," he said, pointing at the tree under whose branches he had just prayed. "That's our lodgepole for the Sun Dance. It's the right size and strength. When the time comes, we will cut down this tree." He paused, then said, "The little girl's bones spoke to me. She wants to be buried. We need to bury her. We need to return her bones to the earth. As long as she is contained in a museum display case, she is still wandering. She is not home with her parents, her grandparents, and her people. I will take this request to a council of our entire tribe. I will recommend that we participate in the reenactment but only on one condition. The museum and the townspeople must give us the bones of the little girl killed in the attack."

Luke was impressed. He didn't speak. He just closed his eyes and bowed his head in respect. The two men turned their backs on the Washita and walked up the path on ground gently rising from the river. Along fence posts and from tree branches hung small amulets of tobacco wrapped in calico cloth. Luke remembered coming to the Washita as a child. He remembered his mother and father hanging amulets on the tree branches and watching them sing to the four directions. Until now he had never joined them. What could he give to the place, what could he leave as an offering?

He stopped and sang. This time it was Two Feathers who stood apart, watching his nephew give his voice to the four directions and to the wind, watching him sing to seek inspiration and to heal the land. After he finished they silently walked back to the truck. When they reached the truck, Two Feathers heaved his body behind the steering wheel, sighed, and said, "It remains to be seen whether the tribe will agree to this plan. Whatever the decision, it will not be an easy one."

Luke remarked thoughtfully, "Funny how our history stays with us and continues to shape our present and future." The men drove away on the black ribbon of road undulating over the gentle hills, away from the sun, now beginning to sink toward the horizon.

Chapter Twenty

≈

Clinton, Oklahoma

DOLORES WHITE CALF squatted on the floor of the church. A thin, birdlike woman with an incongruous round face, she sat cross-legged. She could feel the cold linoleum of the church floor chilling her thighs and seeping through the thin quilt patches she moved around in an intersecting kaleidoscope of colors. Which ones should she choose for the quilt?

Before long the other quilters would drive into the small parking lot, slamming car doors and laughing. They would instantly transform the quiet church into a hive of activity. Older women with armloads of fabric would join young, stay-at-home mothers with small children and babies. They would spread out thousands of colored blocks on the tabletops and overspill to the floor, where the older women preferred to work. Some in the group would bring bean soup, fry bread, and coffee, food now considered traditional to her people. Women brought their babies and food but also an eagerness to discuss issues personal and public and an opportunity to share their lives with one another.

Dolores preferred to come to the quilting circle early. She enjoyed the silence and the smells of the church she had attended since before her memory started. She breathed in the solitude and gave thanks for it. Her life as a mother, auntie, and *nahaa'e* was full, with rarely a moment to spare. As she continued to sort the colors she chortled to herself. She knew the men in her town were well aware of how many issues were discussed and decided during this weekly quilting session. The women who attended the circle wielded a great deal of influence. How many town council and tribal decisions were the results of pillow talk following the discussion at the quilting circle?

Her attention was drawn back to the colorful patches. Now would be a good time, while it was still quiet, to focus on choosing the dominant colors and the pattern for her next quilt. She frowned. The colors before her reminded her of something, but she couldn't quite put her mind to it. Brilliant red stripes offset deep yellows and bold blacks. She played with the colors of the sacred medicine wheel. Then she remembered where she had seen this color combination before. Someone had placed an old Pendleton wool blanket on the bottom shelf in a row of cabinets lining the room.

She got up, wincing with the pain in her knees as she rose. She slowly walked over to the cabinet and opened the door. There it was. She brought the blanket out into the light and unfolded it. Frowning slightly she walked to the light in the open church door where the sun streamed in. She could tell the blanket was old. It was thick and heavy. The wool fibers had faded over time, but they still spoke of vibrancy and life. The balance of contrasting red, yellow, and black reminded Dolores of the quilt pattern Sun and Shadow, a deliberate contrasting of light and dark colors. Perhaps she could use this old blanket as an inspiration for the pattern of her next quilt.

I could make a star quilt in these colors, she thought. *The contrast of colors would be quite striking.* A quilt started to take shape in her mind. She liked this blanket. She thought about making it into a shawl for the next Sun Dance. First, she would give the blanket a good washing with her special soap made for treating wool. Perhaps a daylong soak in warm water in her bathtub would help to leach out the dust of the ages. Next, to get rid of the ragged edges she would cut the blanket down a size or two. It was far too big for her now and would drag on the ground. Then she would trim it out with a contrasting thread, perhaps red. If she cut it down just a bit and angled it on the bias she could add long fringes. She thought about how fringes swayed when the women danced, like grass in the wind. She could make this old blanket dance again. She laid the blanket on its bias seam and got out her measuring tape. Outside, a car door slammed shut.

"What's that you got there?" Barbara Lean Wolf came near bearing a huge platter of fry bread. Her fry bread was so fragrant it seemed to be still sizzling in the pan.

"This old blanket. I found it here in the cabinets. Any idea where it came from?" Dolores answered.

"No. But it looks so old it must tell a story. I wonder how it got here."

More car doors slammed and in came the women and children. They gathered around Dolores's project, each one fingering and exclaiming about the thick wool and making conjectures about the history of the blanket.

"Pendleton doesn't make thick wool like this anymore."

"You can tell it was once a beautiful blanket. The colors are wonderful."

"I'm thinking about making a star quilt using these colors. I've gathered the colors on the floor over there." Dolores pointed to her circle of squares.

"Yes, let's do that," the women quickly agreed. "It will be nice to have a quilt and a matching shawl. Would you consider selling them as a pair at our next fund-raiser?" Before Dolores could answer another car door slammed outside.

"Oh good, it must be Eleanor with the bean soup. My little ones, after we come here, that's all they want to eat," one of the mothers joked.

To the women's surprise, Two Feathers and Luke walked in.

Dolores was pleased to see Luke. He was a favorite friend of her boys. They would be glad to hear that he was back in town.

Luke saw Dolores looking at him. "Hi, Dolores. I've come home for spring break. I'm helping my uncle build a buffalo fence."

Dolores joked, "Buffalo! I would think with your riding ability it would be horses."

"Uncle wants buffalo, says they are more authentic to the traditional Cheyenne way of life."

"I guess my boys will be rounding up buffalo for Mary then. There are not many fences that can keep those animals in."

"Yeah. It is likely my *nahaa'e* will need their help, especially when Two Feathers is out of town. Two Feathers . . ." Luke paused. "Two Feathers has something to say to the circle."

Two Feathers began, "I saw your cars parked outside and remembered that today is the sewing-circle meeting. I have something important to ask the women of the tribe. If the women say we should proceed with what I have to ask, then I will ask the tribal elders for their approval. If you don't think we should honor this request, then I will proceed no further."

Dolores and Barbara exchanged glances. Dolores put down her scissors and crossed her arms over her chest. She was ready to listen. Two Feathers told the assembled women about his discussion with the museum director and how the little girl's bones spoke to him.

As Two Feathers related the museum director's request, the women gradually moved, quite unconsciously, into a circle, some standing and some sitting, but all coming in close to hear his soft-spoken words. It was then that Dolores noticed how tired Two Feathers looked. He and Luke looked as if they carried the weight of the world into the circle. His news was met with a stunned silence. To Luke it felt as if they were silent for a very long time. The silence was not a silence of condemnation. Rather, it was a silence of thoughtfulness. Each pondered what she could say that would add wisdom to what seemed like a momentous decision. Finally, Barbara Lean Wolf said, "This action is not something I would ask for, but we can do this to honor our ancestors who died in the massacre. If my sisters agree, tell the museum director we will participate only if the bones are returned. Our little *nahaa'e*'s bones must go home to her mother the earth. When her bones return to the earth, she can return to the spirit world, join her family, and be born again. Are we agreed?" The others nodded.

One of the oldest women in the group addressed Dolores. "We should use that old wool blanket. Dolores, you're the best designer among us. Remake that blanket into a shawl for her. We'll all help with the star quilt. Let's make the star quilt and the shawl for the little girl. She'll need a shawl and a star quilt in her next life. She's been cold long enough."

A young girl spoke up. "Oh, Mama. The quilt and shawl will be so pretty. Why would you want to bury the little girl in beautiful things you just made?"

Luke added, "I agree. Use your sewing talents to raise money for our schools and hospitals. I understand wanting to bury these bones. She needs a proper burial. But honestly, she's been dead for a hundred years, what difference will a burial shawl and quilt make? She won't know."

Dolores replied, "It is the Cheyenne way to bury women in their raw-hide dresses. That's why there are so few old rawhide dresses around. We don't do that anymore, at least not much. Burying the bones in a shawl and quilt made especially for her upholds the tradition. It's true that she won't be buried in a rawhide dress, but a thick woolen shawl is a good way to keep to the spirit of the tradition. Buffalo robes are hard to come by these days. Since the women of the tribe will work on it, this star quilt will be just as sacred as a buffalo robe."

Luke remained quiet. For once his skeptical questions were answered to his contentment.

Chapter Twenty-One

Clinton, Oklahoma

ALL THROUGH THE summer and into the fall small groups of people gathered in Two Feathers's workshop. They prepared a coffin for the little girl. After much deliberation Two Feathers purchased planks of Osage orange, the strongest wood on the plains. He had the wood planed and sanded at a nearby mill. Then, praying as he built the coffin, he made a simple wooden box. Sheets of bronze were ordered from Oklahoma City. When the bronze arrived, the men gathered. They hammered the sheets of bronze, creating small circular dents in an even pattern. They cut the sheets to size and attached them to Two Feathers's wood box. Then they pounded brass rivets along the seams and the joints of the box. Along the lid and top of the casket, they pressed circles, symbols of the Great Medicine Wheel and the renewal of life.

The women of the tribe padded the coffin and lined it with soft fabric. Small amulets containing sacred herbs, tobacco, and grasses were sewn together and laid in the bottom of the box. They laid the baby quilt, cut and pieced in the shape of a star, into the small coffin and arranged it so that when the time came it would cradle the little *nahaa'e*'s bones. The quilt sang in colors of vibrant red, deep yellows, stark white, and the darkest black. Over the coffin the women draped the shawl. Dolores had worked hard to remake the blanket into a shawl and she had decorated it with long red fringes.

When the coffin was prepared, Two Feathers called the director and told him he was ready to pick up the bones. On a cool fall day, Two Feathers again drove the fifty miles to Cheyenne. There he took the bones of the little girl and, one by one, praying over them, he gently and reverently placed them in the bronze coffin. He left the museum with the bones. He felt the sun on his face and the Oklahoma wind blowing around his ears. She was almost home.

Just as he was ready to put the coffin in the front seat of his truck, the museum director called out to him from the door of the museum. "I hope we still have a deal. Your tribe will participate in the reenactment, right?"

Two Feathers turned, still holding the bronze-covered coffin. "We will be there."

"And you'll set up tipis along the Washita?" The museum director seemed worried that Two Feathers would not honor their arrangement.

"We are prepared to set up our tipis."

"It would be really great if those buffalo I hear you're bringing up from Texas could somehow be there. Buffalo would make it so much more real. How many do have at your place so far?"

Two Feathers paused and answered with difficulty, "Eight." He paused again. "What do you know about buffalo?"

"I've read all about them. Why?"

"Have you ever worked with them?"

"Don't know that I've ever seen one in person."

"Buffalo are not like cows," Two Feathers patiently explained. "You can't manage them."

"Really?" The museum director did not sound convinced.

"They can clear a six-foot fence."

"Okay." The director seemed convinced on the point about the buffalo. "So buffalo are out. What about horses? Could you bring horses and tether them in the cottonwood groves along the river?"

"Horses are expensive. We can only supply tipis and tribal people. No horses." Two Feathers was becoming impatient though he tried not to show it.

The museum director persisted with his agenda. "Everyone will be in Native costume, right?" Two Feathers sighed and looked at the museum director, his exasperation starting to show itself in the set of his mouth. The director finally began to take stock of his situation with Two Feathers and modified his request. "At least some of you will be in Native costume, right? Your women could wear their fancy powwow dresses."

Two Feathers paused. He had not realized that the townspeople would take the reenactment this far. He turned away from the director and placed the coffin in the front seat of his truck. When he turned toward the director he chose his words carefully. "Women don't wear plain rawhide dresses anymore. Most of our Native clothing is highly decorated. The women spend months beading and decorating their dresses. Just to get the leather to the point where it's pliable takes a tremendous amount of work. Most women buy their leather from a supplier. They don't cure it themselves. It's expensive to purchase this type of leather. By the time our women are finished with a dress it is truly a work of art. I doubt they'll want to wear something that special for a reenactment of a bad story. They usually save their dresses for happier times: powwows, weddings, tribal celebrations, and dances. Most of the men will want to wear jeans. You might get a few men looking more like cowboys than Indians."

A slight frown crossed the museum director's face.

"We had hoped for your full cooperation, Two Feathers. You have the bones. We would like pageantry, display, a sense of history. It would be nice to have a real, full-size Indian village. That's what we are advertising. That's what our paying customers will want to see."

Both men were now impatient with each other. Trying to mollify the director, Two Feathers decided to insert some humor, or at least a small bit of sense into the deteriorating situation. "When did the attack happen?" he asked.

"At dawn."

"Do you know, was Black Kettle's band dressed in traditional regalia at that point in the day? Most Indians do not wear traditional clothing to bed, although it's been said that one of our great-grandmothers was so traumatized by Sand Creek and the Washita that she wore her moccasins to bed. If you want an accurate depiction of the massacre, my people should be dressed in simple clothing or nude. I'll do what I can, but I doubt that any requests for powwow dresses will be honored. Southern Cheyennes do not march in lockstep with their leaders. They listen closely and make their own decisions. My people have agreed to participate in your reenactment so that the bones of the little girl will finally be returned to her people. She deserves to rest. After she is returned to the earth her spirit will join those of her parents and grandparents." Two Feathers spoke with great dignity and feeling.

The director heard the sorrow in his voice and noticed his conciliatory manner. "Okay. I understand that you'll do what you can. I'll be in touch about this."

"Fine. I'll expect your call." Two Feathers's short answer indicated that he knew there was little more to say.

That evening in the back office of the Black Kettle Museum the museum director opened a letter from the Grandsons of the Seventh Cavalry. It read, "As the captain of the Grandsons of the Seventh Cavalry I would like to thank you for contacting us. I've discussed your request with my men. We would be all too happy to participate in the reenactment of the Battle of the Washita. Will it be held on November 27, the one hundredth anniversary of the battle? Please let us know how we can assist your town with the reenactment. Most of us live in California. If you want men and horses to muster we will need some time to make arrangements and to provide transportation for the men and animals. Any assistance you could provide with research and information would be helpful. We take our reenactment responsibilities seriously and hope to sustain rather than contradict the historical record. Sincerely, Walter Smith."

The museum director folded the letter in half and tucked it into his shirt pocket. He smiled, his former conciliatory stance evaporating. *Now things are beginning to shape up*, he thought. *Now we can have a real reenactment and I won't have to go begging for horses from Two Feathers. Those Cheyennes are in for a big surprise.*

Chapter Twenty-Two

Washita

TWO FEATHERS PUSHED his chair away from the table. "Now *that* was a good Thanksgiving Day meal. Thank you, Mary." Two Feathers's wife, Mary, smiled at him from across the table. She had done a wonderful job of preparing the typical meal of stuffed turkey, green beans, sweet potatoes, and stuffing. To the menu she had added dried buffalo meat heavily seasoned and reconstituted in a flavorful broth, Indian fry bread, bean soup, and rich, dark coffee. "I'm glad we decided to celebrate Thanksgiving early this year. This weekend is such a full one. You have a tough job this afternoon setting up the Indian camp, and I wanted to feed both your stomach and your soul. You'll need your strength."

"I guess you women have made enough food to feed the tribe after the reenactment?"

"Yes, everything is in Crock-Pots and large casserole dishes. Margie's bringing the venison. Eleanor's bringing her famous beans, and Barbara's bringing her fry bread. I have rice pudding and corn salad ready. It's keeping cool on your workbench in the garage. We have a lot of food to transport out there."

"This should be an interesting Thanksgiving, with the reenactment tomorrow morning. It reminds me that this truly is a time of giving thanks for us," Two Feathers mused.

"You mean to say we are giving thanks for still being here, right?" Luke looked at his *naxane* in consternation. He was not happy. The old man gave in too much. He remembered with resentment the day the museum director made his pitch for the reenactment.

"Why do we have to bend over backward to get back what is rightfully ours? Maybe we should rename Thanksgiving. Let's call it 'Survivors Day' and give thanks that we're still here, especially when I consider what you have planned."

Two Feathers noticed Luke's riding trophies in the living room and made a mental note that this young man, his hotheaded, passionate nephew, had channeled his energy in positive ways. Two Feathers had deliberately displayed the trophies. The trophies honored Luke and reminded Two Feathers of his responsibilities as a Cheyenne uncle. "Yes, I mean to say I am grateful to finally have the little girl's bones back. I am grateful that Magpie and Big Hawk survived, and that our culture and our people have come back from the brink of extinction. I also mean to say I am grateful for Black Kettle's and White Antelope's visions of peace. And, for future generations, I am grateful for those who choose to be guided by these stories."

"You put too much emphasis on peace. Geronimo fought back and he lived. Sitting Bull fought back and went on to make money in the Buffalo Bill shows. Lots of men fought back and survived. I don't see what the big deal is."

Two Feathers relented. "I understand you aren't interested in the peace position required of a Southern Cheyenne peace chief. Still, I hope you will agree to set up the tipis and participate in the reenactment. We need tribal members from your age group to join us. It will be an opportunity for you to participate in the life of the tribe and learn a little bit about your history."

Luke countered, "I know all about my history. Big Hawk and the Kiowa, Eonah-pah, fought back. I know the stories. They survived. I'll help out with this reenactment of yours because you're my uncle and I wanted to get those bones back. Just don't expect me to like it."

Mary looked at Two Feathers and smiled. "He reminds me of someone I knew long ago."

Two Feathers responded ruefully, "Some of us mellow with age."

Mary teased her husband, "That's another thing to give thanks for."

Two Feathers smiled at her but then directed his words to Luke. "It's well past noon and we have a tipi to set up. When you're ready, Luke, we'll all go."

Two Feathers, Mary, and Luke drove out to the Washita battlefield site. Along with other members of the tribe, they planned to set up their tipis near the banks of the river. It had started to snow and Two Feathers could feel the temperature dropping. The Washita was frozen over, but Two Feathers could hear it gurgling under the thin layer of ice. He shivered. Luke noticed and remarked, "Seems the weather is cooperating with the reenactment, too."

Most of the camp had already been built by the time they got there. Younger children ran around the camp, playing tag and hide-and-seek and eating fry bread and meat from the fires that the women tended. There was much excitement and nervous energy. The children joked about pretending to be dead. How many times would they stagger and clutch at their hearts before tripping over in mock defeat?

Dolores White Calf walked briskly toward Two Feathers and Luke, her two sons trailing behind. "We've saved a spot for you near the middle of the camp, just outside the center circle. You're the peace chief; your place is near the center."

"My clan always raises their tipis on the west side of the circle. Oral tradition tells us that Medicine Woman Later's lodge was on the edge of camp, not near the center," Two Feathers responded.

Mary spoke up. "I don't like being the center of attention. Do we have to camp so close to the center?"

Dolores answered, "I knew you wouldn't like the arrangement. Since this is supposed to be 1868, that's where the peace chief's tipi would be, near the center, not the edge. I don't know why Medicine Woman Later's tipi was at the edge of the camp. Since we are trying to teach the next generation about tribal ways, I would prefer to raise your tipi in the center even though that's not historically accurate."

Mary nodded appreciatively at Dolores and then sighed. "If Two Feathers is Black Kettle's stand-in, I guess I'm Medicine Woman Later's in this instance. I'll camp near the center of the circle as you planned. I hope they don't expect me to reenact her death and fall into the Washita River. It's a bit cold for that."

Dolores responded, "You're right. These townspeople have no idea what they're putting us through, expecting us to remember these bad stories. It isn't easy."

Luke asked Dolores, "When do you expect the townspeople will come running through the camp yelling and pretending to attack us? It looks like the kids are already having fun with this."

"Yes, and thank goodness they are. They seem to treat this like a big game. As for the attack," Dolores replied, "the Seventh Cavalry struck at dawn. I'm sure the townspeople will want to reenact it as accurately as possible."

She turned toward Mary. "Where do you think we should put the coffin?"

Mary reflected. "I think we should move her to the middle of the circle. That's her place now. She is the reason for our being here. She belongs in the highest place of honor."

"Good point. It's getting late. The sun's about to set and there'll be dancing in the village tonight." Turning her attention to her boys she called, "This tipi isn't going to go up by itself. Hey you two, stop standing around watching. We need your help."

"Mom, that's women's work. The Indian man's job is to watch the women work," Nathan teased his mother.

"When you start bringing home meat for my table, then you can stand around and watch. Until then, your job is to help your mother," Dolores retorted. "Second, the reason I can't set up this tipi by myself is because I don't do it that much anymore and those poles are heavy. Setting up a tipi doesn't come automatically and, in case you didn't notice, these tipis don't come with instruction manuals."

Nathan and Kevin shuffled over to Dolores's side and eyed the tipi poles and canvas cloth dubiously. Kevin addressed Luke. "Your tipi doesn't look authentic. Did your *nahaa'e* buy it from the Sears and Roebuck catalog?"

"This tipi?" Luke jested back. "Nah, this tipi is a fine original Craftsman home."

"Ah, you mean you received all the materials and sewed it together yourself!" Nathan said, laughing.

"Absolutely. My family got together and sewed it while I was away at college." Luke grunted as he balanced a lodgepole into place.

"How did the women do it, Dolores? Either we've lost the art of setting up tipis or our grandmothers were Amazons. Family lore has it that Medicine Woman Later could strike a tipi in less time than it takes to saddle a horse. Seems unbelievable."

"Well, they had to. You know they were always on the move either chasing buffalo or being chased by the army. Being ready to go at a moment's notice was important. The life of the tribe depended on it. Don't forget how important women's work was to the tribe. You men may have provided the meat, but we women made every item the tribe used in daily life. I sometimes think we've gotten so soft that we've lost our way. Now come on, boys." She cajoled her sons, "Luke will have the whole thing up before you even lift a finger."

Two Feathers approached Luke and the boys. "When you're done with that, I have a task for us, and we need to complete it before tomorrow morning. I want to cut down the Sun Dance tree, the strong cottonwood that stands by the Washita, and use it as the flagpole in the middle of the camp. It is said that Black Kettle flew a US flag and a white flag. We'll do that too. It's a way to make the statement that his band was peaceful and was still cut down in cold blood."

Luke grimaced. "Soon as we're done I'll help. I'll get my tools from the pickup and join you. Are you coming with us?" He turned toward Nathan and Kevin.

"I'm always happy to teach whites Indian history." Nathan grinned. "We're in."

<hr />

Two Feathers and the young men walked along the Washita, choosing to walk through the tall, rustling grass by the banks instead of taking the easier, higher path that had been mowed the day before. As they walked the winds shifted, the temperature suddenly dropped, and the night sky seemed brighter and clearer. At the Washita the trees shimmered in the silvery light. Their shadowy outlines against the snow were stark and twisted. One tree stood tall above the others. It was not a perfect tree. Its top branches were already broken off.

"That's our tree. It will make a great flagpole. We won't need to do much work to prepare it," Luke observed. "I wonder how old it is. I wonder if it saw the massacre, back in 1868." A slight breeze gently shook the tree's branches. Luke looked closely at the tree. Was the tree talking to him? Was it answering his questions? Two Feathers caught Luke's astonished look and smiled at him with a knowing glance.

Chapter Twenty-Three

Washita

THE SKY WAS just starting to lighten as Dolores gathered her children, nieces, and nephews for one last talk before the reenactment began. A small fire burned in the center of the tipi. Instead of dressing her children in traditional clothing, Dolores had opted for modern clothing, long johns, thick woolen pants, double layers of socks, boots, hats, mittens, and heavy padded jackets. She wasn't willing to sacrifice her children's health for this reenactment even though she had wanted the bones back just as much as Two Feathers.

Dolores White Calf began, "Think of how our people used to sleep in these tipis, everyone crowded together. This is a large tipi but still, they lived most of their lives out in the open."

"Hey, Mom," Nathan said, sticking his head inside the tent flap, "I think the reenactment is about to begin. I can see cars and people standing on the ridge above the river. It seems folks have gathered."

Dolores turned toward the children gathered around her. "You know this is an important day in the history of our tribe. We know from the stories we've heard what happened that day. What will we do when the townspeople come running through the camp?"

"Run and hide in the grass!" shouted one of her nieces.

"That is a good plan. Run and hide. Just get out of the way. Okay?"

"And why are we doing this?" she asked her children, wanting to make sure they understood the significance of the day.

"So we can bury the bones of the little girl who died in the massacre."

"That's right. This is something we are doing so that she can be properly buried. We do not want our little *nahaa'e* to wander forever. She must be buried so she can join our people on the other side. Let's stay still and see if we can hear the townspeople. When they start yelling and running through the camp, we'll run."

The ground was covered with blankets and small cots. Dolores's family settled down. They hushed one another and waited in anticipation of the attack. The little ones looked at their aunt with wide eyes. To them it felt kind of like playing hide-and-seek.

Behind a hill just north of the Washita, Walter Smith shifted uncomfortably in his saddle. For once he had done his research and he was no longer feeling quite so positive about his participation in the reenactment. He had read how Black Kettle was a highly decorated peace chief, one who had signed peace treaties and kept his promises. He read how Black Kettle flew both a white flag for peace and a US flag in his village, declaring his allegiance to the United States. He knew that President Lincoln had bestowed a peace medal on Black Kettle during the peace chief's visit to the nation's capital. In the village below him Walter could see the two flags flying. The US flag whipped in the wind over a huge white flag. Walter looked at the size of the white flag and knew someone down there knew Black Kettle's history too. Someone was making a point with that huge white flag. Walter knew that Custer claimed to have killed 103 warriors but that Black Kettle's village was sworn to peace and that, in fact, most of those killed were women and children. He had also read about how Black Kettle and his wife, Medicine Woman Later, had survived the horrific Sand Creek Massacre four years before the one at Washita.

"What am I doing? What the hell am I doing?" All of a sudden he wanted to turn his horse around and ride west, back to California. He wanted to ride without stopping.

He looked up and down the line of sixty men who had agreed to come with him. They were smartly dressed in exact replicas of US Army indigo-blue uniforms. The sun's rays bounced off brass buttons and highly polished leather boots. Much time, effort, and money had been expended to make their uniforms, saddles, guns, insignias, flags, everything as authentic as possible. Then his eyes widened. *So much for authenticity*, he thought. Some of the younger men who thought very highly of themselves were wearing sunglasses.

"Hey you wise guys, take off those glasses," he barked. "In 1868 the US Army did not supply sunglasses. Sunglasses were not standard issue."

All of the Grandsons apologetically and quickly obeyed their commanding officer and took off their sunglasses. All except one complied. Walter saw who it was, grimaced, and broke rank to ride and confront the lone dissenter. "Listen, Mack, you've challenged my command every step of the way. You aren't worthy of participating in this reenactment. Take off those glasses or you'll sit this one out."

Mack sat casually on his horse. The horse's coat gleamed from brushing and the saddle shone with polish. Clearly, he took very good care of his horse and tack. Mack's personal appearance, though, was definitely substandard for a Seventh Cavalry man. He was scruffy and his uniform was wrinkled and smudged with food stains. He presented poorly and looked out of place alongside the other neatly pressed and dressed Grandsons. On the side of the saddle Walter noticed that Mack had attached a small replica of a Confederate flag.

"What's that on your saddle?" Walter asked with exasperation. "Custer was an officer for the Union. He didn't fight for the Confederacy. What are you thinking?"

"It's just my way of making a statement, sir," Mack drawled.

"Well, it isn't regulation. There's no way the US Army would have issued a Confederate flag, especially just three years after the Civil War ended. Get rid of it." Walter's voice became harsher with every word.

"Won't come off . . . sir. It's glued on good and proper." Mack made no attempt to hide his sarcasm. "I'll take my shades off. That should be good enough for you."

"I'm not going to fight you here." Walter pointed his finger at Mack. "You just do as I say."

Mack took his glasses off with a sneer and stuffed them into his shirt. "Guess we'll see about that, Grandpa."

Witnessing this exchange was a group of teenagers. They were the sons of the Grandsons. Their fathers were on horseback, but they were on foot and carried bugles and drums. They called themselves Custer's Pride. The sons of the Grandsons had rehearsed Custer's battle tune, "Garryowen," and were eager to play it. Among the trumpet players was Walter's son. His son looked up at him. Walter knew what his son was thinking. His son had often asked him why they needed to bring Mack along. Walter had patiently explained that Mack was a descendent of a Seventh Cavalry officer and as such had automatic admittance into their membership.

"We're waiting. Seems everything is ready. Make the call, Captain Dad." His son's encouraging voice calmed him and he took a deep breath. All eyes were on him. He knew it was too late to turn back so he gave the command, "Troops at the ready." He paused and then yelled, "Charge!" Out of the corner of his eye he saw his son raise his bugle to his lips and begin the opening strains of the drinking song.

⚊⚊

Outside the tipi below in the village Nathan heard a strange sound coming from behind the hills. At first he thought it was the wind, then he thought he heard a train whistle, but that also was not quite right. As the sounds came closer he heard bugles and snare drums. Someone was playing a cavalry charge. He heard the sounds of horses' hooves, thudding in unison on the cold, hard ground, galloping in formation. As he looked up he saw troops cresting the low ridge of the hills. His consternation turned to fear as horses ridden by men in uniform poured over the hill. He thrust his head through the tipi's door flap and said, "Something's wrong. There are real soldiers coming to get us. Run. I mean it. Run. There are real troops. Get the kids out of here."

Dolores looked up in alarm, ran out of the tent, and gasped. "You," she said, pointing at one of her older nieces, "run to tall grass and hide. Take the little ones with you. Don't come out until you hear me calling your name. Go." The children ran toward the reeds and rushes but not before the Grandsons of the Seventh Cavalry streamed into the village. Dolores saw their military uniforms and their bright brass buttons. When she saw their long pointed sabers held high above their heads, she almost fainted in horror. The Grandsons pointed their carbines at the Cheyenne men, women, and children. Loud bangs from blanks in the guns went off in rapid-fire succession, in a series of ominous staccatos. Nathan could hear townspeople on the ridge overlooking the village cheering for the cavalry.

Luke burst out of his tipi and into the mayhem. What he saw made him shake with anger. The village scene was chaotic. With no weapons, no way to protect their families, the men of the village did all they could. They ran to stand between the women and children. Cavalry men chased down women and children on horseback. Others tied ropes to poles and started to pull down the tipis, deliberately destroying them. Tipi poles cracked and snapped as one by one the tipis came down. Luke wished he had brought his gun along. He would have loaded it in a heartbeat; only his bullets would be the real thing, not these toy blanks. A cavalry reenactor circled his horse through the camp, each time coming dangerously close to some children, one of whom had scurried under a wagon. On the reenactor's saddle Luke saw a gleaming replica of the Confederate flag. *God, these guys are idiots*, thought Luke. As Luke watched the soldier galloping through the camp he remembered the story of Eonah-pah, how he had shot an officer in the stomach and grabbed his horse. Luke's practiced eye watched the horse's movements. As the man circled around again Luke ran behind him and lunged at the rider. It was a risky move, calculated to surprise his opponent but also putting Luke in the path of a potentially fatal kick from a loyal horse. Luke's years of training and riding paid off. With a wild yell Luke pulled the soldier off his horse and began beating him. As Mack fell to the ground he covered his face with his hands and rolled into a ball.

"You white asshole," Luke swore over and over as he beat and kicked Mack.

Two Feathers ran to Luke. He pulled Luke off Mack, who lay on the ground moaning. He shook him and backed him up against the wagon. "Stop this. You will create a real battle and we are completely outnumbered." He grabbed the horse's reins. Mack rolled on the ground, tried to sit up, and fell back down. Steadying Mack's mount, Two Feathers spoke urgently to Luke. "Now get out of here. Ride away. Save yourself. These guys in blue mean business. They will not let this go. They will hunt you down."

"No. I'm staying and I'm fighting these white assholes. I'm fighting them."

Two Feathers yelled at Luke. "With what? Don't you fight. Don't fight."

Two Feathers shocked himself. He had never yelled at Luke before. He took a couple of deep breaths and then moderated his tone. "If you fight, you will only make things worse for us. You know the story of White Antelope?"

"Yes, I do," Luke replied somewhat sarcastically. "I know the story of White Antelope. He sang instead of fighting, and look what happened to him."

Two Feathers spoke earnestly. "Sing with me. If you won't ride away, stay with me. Sing with me instead of fighting."

Two Feathers dropped the reins and raised both hands in the air. Standing and turning toward the four directions he sang out in a clear, strong voice. He felt the wind carry his song into the grass where the children hid, into the village where the whites and Indians faced off, and onto the ridge where the townspeople stood watching. Dolores ran from her hiding place, ululating as loud as she possibly could, and joined Two Feathers. Barbara, Mary, Nathan, parents, and elders joined in, circled, faced the sacred directions, and sang. Raising their hands, they protested with their voices this latest deliberate, nightmarish act of violence to be visited upon their people.

Luke's breath slowed. As he stood and watched the singing circle take shape, his mind cleared. He took two steps into the circle and joined his kinsman, his band, his tribe. In that instant he knew how his uncle, grandfather, and forefathers and mothers had negotiated between the worlds of Native and white. He knew how his uncle had lived in the circle but carried the cross. His uncle had done it through deliberate nonviolence. He had survived by refusing to do violence to either side. Luke knew he might not be able to follow his uncle's path in all instances, but in this one he raised his voice and sang a prayer for strength from the northwest, clarity from the northeast, calmness from the southeast, resolution from the southwest.

Walter stopped his horse and motioned to the others to stop as well. One by one the Grandsons in blue stopped riding through the village. The strains of "Garryowen" died away as the men in blue looked in astonishment at the Cheyennes singing, singing for their lives.

Chapter Twenty-Four

Washita

TWO FEATHERS REALIZED his hands were still clenched in anger. How could the Grandsons of the Seventh Cavalry have done this? Why hadn't the museum director and the white townspeople told him they were coming? He turned toward the elderly chiefs. As peace chief he was expected to remain calm, yet his stomach roiled and his heart burned.

The singers were gathered close together and the circle had become tighter. Gradually the singing stopped. A horse snorted and stomped his hoof. A hush came over the camp. Only the wind in the trees was heard. Two Feathers could feel the people looking at him. They were looking for leadership. They were looking for him to find a way out of this awful situation, but he was still so angry. The singing had settled the mock battle, but emotions ran high. After a few more moments of silence in which Two Feathers struggled to maintain composure, one of the elders spoke up. "You are peace chief. You must end this bad story."

"How? I do not have a path." Two Feathers felt hopeless.

"You will find a path." Two Feathers turned toward where the Grandsons of the Seventh Cavalry had gathered. His footsteps fell heavily on the snow, and as he walked toward them he had no idea what he could possibly say to them.

Dolores White Calf stepped forward. "I know the way," she said. "Follow me."

Dolores led Two Feathers and the elders to the bronze coffin, set in the middle of the camp. Miraculously, the coffin remained unharmed. It sat in

155

the middle of the circle, the shawl still draped over it. She took the beautiful shawl from where she had placed it. The colors of the shawl danced in the dazzling winter sunlight. She talked quietly to Two Feathers and the small circle of elders.

"Too many times our people have heard 'Garryowen.' We've heard hoof beats coming to massacre us. I do not want my children to hear the drums and the bugle. This shawl was draped over a coffin. Now it is sacred. Tradition says it must be given away to the most honored guest. Two Feathers, it is up to you. Go and give this sacred shawl to the Grandsons of the Seventh Cavalry. Give it as a gift of peace so that they will never again attack us. Do you agree?" She addressed the elders who, one by one, solemnly nodded approval.

Two Feathers trembled. His hands shook but he remembered when his elderly *naxane* told stories about Black Kettle. He remembered how Black Kettle had tried to make peace with whites. He knew the elders of his tribe wanted him to make peace. He was profoundly grateful that Dolores White Calf had shown him a way through his anger. He took the shawl Dolores had made and walked toward the leader of the Grandsons of the Seventh Cavalry.

As Two Feathers approached the place where the Grandsons of the Seventh Cavalry sat on their horses he heard the words, "Present arms."

The Grandsons unsheathed their swords in an act of homage, a salute, to Two Feathers.

Two Feathers did not share their perspective. To him the salute was an outrage. How could they salute him with the very weapons that had been used to kill his people one hundred years earlier? His steps faltered and he turned back and looked at his band gathered behind him. He stood for what seemed like a very long time.

Dolores stepped forward to join him. Mary, Luke, and the elders, men and women, walked up to him in a show of support.

The group approached Walter Smith.

Two Feathers took a deep breath before speaking. "You are the captain of the Grandsons?"

"I am."

"Place it on his shoulders," Dolores said.

Two Feathers addressed Walter. "I ask you to stand down so that I may present you with this gift."

Walter swung out of his saddle and faced Two Feathers, his eyes full of questions.

"Turn around," Two Feathers said. Walter turned his back to Two Feathers. In a gesture of respect and honor Two Feathers reached over and very carefully placed Magpie's blanket around the leader's shoulders.

Two Feathers said to Walter, "You may not know this about our culture. This is a most sacred shawl. It covered the bones of a little girl who died in the Washita Massacre one hundred years ago. We want your people never to attack us again. This is why we are honoring you with the shawl. Keep it as a reminder of a strong people who have forgiven you and who wish to live in peace."

Walter's eyes welled up with tears as he said, "Your people have heard 'Garryowen' and the drums of the Seventh Cavalry. I promise you we will play them no more. We will not attack you again. You are safe."

Dolores White Calf quietly said, "This is good."

Mary spoke to Walter. "As the peace chief's wife, the one in the tribe who offers hospitality, I would like to honor your men and the townspeople with a meal. The women of our tribe prepared a traditional Indian meal for when the reenactment was over. There is enough for all of us. Please join us. We are serving this meal in the small church in town . . . You know, the one that has burritos on the menu?" She smiled, and in her smile and invitation she released the tension of the moment.

Walter smiled back, relieved. "It's one of the only restaurants in town. Thank you. I'll tell my men."

The Cheyennes, the museum director, the townspeople, and the Seventh Cavalry sat down to share a meal. Two Feathers waited until all the soldiers, all the townspeople, and all the Cheyennes had started eating. Luke waited with him. Two Feathers could sense Luke was still shaking inside from the events of the day. He put his hand on Luke's shoulder to help calm him. "Let's eat."

"I can't," Luke replied tersely. "My stomach is in knots. I'm still too mad."

As Two Feathers approached the buffet he noticed Walter helping Dolores to the table. Walter pulled out a chair for Dolores and she smiled in return. Walter and the Grandsons sat down with the Cheyennes. They began to engage in awkward table conversation and slowly the room filled with the sounds of eating and talking.

Mack came to the table, his plate heaping with food, his face bruised where Luke had punched him.

"Satisfied, you red son of a bitch?" he taunted Luke.

"I'll be satisfied when your people leave my people alone," Luke retorted.

Kevin and Nathan walked to Luke's side, their faces grim. They faced Mack, bodies tense and features implacable, ready to defend their friend.

Walter jerked back his chair and with a loud bang it fell to the floor. Swiping at his mouth with a napkin before throwing it on the floor behind him, he approached Mack. Walter reminded Two Feathers of a caged lion, barely able to contain his energy. Walter whispered into Mack's ear; his face was set in deep, furrowed lines and his jaw was rigid. He took Mack's plate from him, set it on the table, and then motioned for him to leave. After a moment of tense indecision Mack left the room with Walter following him, ready to pounce and glaring at Mack's every step until he was gone. Luke retrieved Walter's chair and placed it upright. He looked at Two Feathers. Two Feathers could see his nephew was still angry, but at least he was civil. At least he acknowledged what Walter had just done. After Walter closed the door behind Mack he returned to his plate of food and sat down. Dolores bent down and retrieved his discarded napkin—a second quiet gesture of appreciation.

Slowly Two Feathers came to the table. He watched the townspeople, the soldiers, and the Cheyennes as they ate traditional Cheyenne food. They dipped fry bread into Indian bean soup and chewed on dried venison soaked in wild berries. Then they passed coffee and rice pudding with raisins across the table to the Grandsons.

As they ate Two Feathers sang a song in his heart. He sang for Black Kettle, who pointed the way to peace. He sang for Medicine Woman Later, who taught the Cheyennes how to listen. He sang for Magpie, who survived to tell the story. He sang for Luke, who stood by him even when he disagreed. He looked at Luke standing with Kevin and Nathan, the young men, like Dog Soldiers, watching the celebration but unable to join it. He sang for them to choose forgiveness and healing. He sang for Dolores White Calf, who showed him how to quiet his anger and how to build with a blanket a new story for his people. He sang a song of gratitude for the wind on the Washita River, whispering still.

Reweaving Magpie's Story

~~~

Acknowledgments and Sources

IN NATIVE AMERICAN culture, grandparents and elders teach the next generation through example and stories. Numerous teachers, storytellers, and guides contributed to this writing in many guises. Cheyenne elders, children, historical accounts, and modern experiences all provided the understanding, knowledge, and inspiration for *Magpie's Blanket*. The insights gleaned, behaviors observed, and speech patterns and ways of living explained provided the threads that wove this story into being.

Peace Chief Lawrence Hart, his wife, Betty, and Raylene Hinz-Penner placed me, a reluctant scholar of Native American women's history, on this path and gave me a gentle nudge. They encouraged me to write a general women's history of the Southern Cheyenne tribe for a conference in 2006. "I'm not trained. I don't have the expertise. I'm not schooled in Native American history," I told them. "We'll help you," was their reply. The first scene in the introduction to this book, that of a peace chief standing on a small hill above the historic massacre site at the Washita River, is drawn from a real experience. Lawrence Hart sang to the four sacred directions and told a small group of Mennonite historians his version of the Washita Massacre. That experience has never left me. It is written on my bones.

Before I knew I was writing a book, this book, Lawrence and Betty opened doors. Elders and bearers of culture consented to be interviewed. Betty Hart again and again gave of her valuable time. She has been a most gracious of hostess over years of visits. Margie Pewo and her family taught me about Cheyenne ways at several Red Moon Powwows. At one of the powwows, I was honored to be a server at a traditional feast in celebration of Margie's granddaughter's first birthday. Interviews and conversations from 2005 to 2008 with Ramona Welch, Oveta Whitehawk, Blanche Hart Whiteshield (and her son Mark Whiteshield, who translated from Cheyenne into English), Lenora Hart Holliman, Emma Standingwater Hart, Joyce Twins, Rita Black, Minoma Littlehawk, and Connie Hart Yellowman added to my understanding of traditional ways and women's lives. Connie's daughter, Christine, is called "Cricket." Her charming name became a character in this book.

More recently, Jennifer A. Whiteman and Dr. Henrietta Mann ensured historical accuracy from a tribal perspective. Jennifer, a lawyer by training and a cultural interpreter by vocation, very carefully read and reread the manuscript. She asked insightful questions, made numerous corrections, and added tribal historical perspectives and nuance. I treasure Jennifer's and Dr. Mann's collaboration and friendship. Both Lawrence Hart and Dr. Mann are direct descendants of massacre survivors. Dr. Mann had a great-grandmother, White Buffalo Woman, who survived both massacres. White Buffalo Woman was about the same age as Magpie in this story. Hart's and Mann's oral histories and family stories provided tribal viewpoints and deeply valuable personal connections to the massacres.

Others lent their support and knowledge to the project. Charles Cambridge, a Navajo scholar, encouraged me to write the book back in 2011 when, at a women's history conference, I tentatively told him about my idea for a historical novel. Again, I wasn't sure I was qualified to write it. His encouraging response was all I needed to continue the project. Since then, conversations with National Park Service rangers Craig Moore at the Sand Creek Massacre National Historic Site and Richard Zahm at the Washita Battlefield National Historic Site have been helpful.

My own family members, aunt Laura Flaming and grandmother Ella Klassen Schmidt, encouraged an appreciation of quilts. Ella's sewing circle, the Willing Helpers at the Alexanderwohl Mennonite Church, sent money and quilting squares to the Hart's church in Clinton, Oklahoma. This delightful discovery, made by my aunt in the Alexanderwohl Church archives, seemed a fortuitous connection and grew into scholarly research on Cheyenne women's sewing societies.

Historians benefit tremendously from the knowledge and expertise of archivists and reference librarians. Elayne Silversmith at the Smithsonian's

National Museum of the American Indian (NMAI) Cultural Resources Center provided valuable assistance, as did John Thiesen and James Lynch, archivists at the Bethel College Mennonite Library and Archives. Symposia and exhibits at the Smithsonian's NMAI illuminated Plains Indian culture and the use of objects in daily life. Numerous grants from Eastern Mennonite University funded research in Oklahoma and Kansas and the presentation of related papers at academic conferences. Eastern Mennonite University staff Erica Grasse and Kelsey Kauffman provided invaluable support. I am the director of a small but intensely active academic program in Washington, DC; Erica and Kelsey ensured that days away from my desk and in the field, at archives and libraries, were productive and hassle-free. Friends from college days, Greta Hiebert and Nathan Smucker, and Mark and Andrea Schmidt Andres, kindly hosted me during several trips to Kansas. Finally, my gratitude, once again, goes to my encouraging friends, especially those in a small group that meets once a month; to my children, Alexander and Bianca Navari; and to my parents, Melvin and Charlotte Schmidt.

I started this journey fully owning my limitations as a scholar of Native American Plains Indian women. Any mistakes in the book are mine, and I would welcome the opportunity to learn from those with more experience and knowledge.

Kimberly D. Schmidt
Hyattsville, MD

~

Much regard, admiration, and appreciation is dedicated to the Cheyenne People who survived, the People from whom my husband and children descend. I thank them for their strength and fortitude, without which I would not have the love and family that I hold so dear. Thank you White Buffalo Woman, thank you Vister, thank you Henrietta Mann. Thank you for your lessons on how to be a proper Cheyenne woman and for permitting me access to your world. Thank you Henrietta for clarifying and answering my numerous questions with patience and grace. Thank you Marc, Aaron, Moriah, and Paige Whiteman for your humor when I need it most. This story is for you and about you, my darlings. And thank you to my mom, Merleen Schott, and dad, Michael Nuhfer, for instilling in me the confidence to step outside my own culture and be open to others. Of course, life wouldn't be the same without the encouragement I constantly receive from Mike Nuhfer, Amy Nuhfer-Degolier, and Doug Nuhfer—you keep me grounded.

Above all, thank you to Alden Whiteman, my crazy, funny husband and confidant. Your ability to put up with my incessant research and chatter is something I so appreciate. Obviously, you must be a little eccentric—just like me.

And finally, thank you to all the Cheyennes yet to come.

Jennifer A. Whiteman
El Reno, Oklahoma

⟿

This story is based on true events and real people. Because there is not enough written documentation about Cheyenne women for the story to stand as historical nonfiction, it was reimagined as fiction. In its general outline the story is true, but many of the characters and details were drawn from oral histories, tribal practices, and historical imagination.

For students who wish to learn more about the Sand Creek and Washita Massacres, nonfiction accounts include George Bird Grinnell, "The Battle of Washita, 1868," in *The Fighting Cheyenne* (Norman: University of Oklahoma Press, 1915, rpt. 1955), 298–309; David Fridtjof Halass and Andrew E. Masich, *Halfbreed: The Remarkable True Story of George Bent— Caught Between the Worlds of the Indian and the White Man* (Cambridge, MA: Da Capo Press, 2005); and Mary Jane Warde, *Washita* (Oklahoma City: Oklahoma Historical Society and the National Park Service, 2003, rpt. 2005). Charles J. Brill gives an impassioned account and provides insights on Black Kettle's philosophy. See Brill, *Custer, Black Kettle, and the Fight on the Washita* (Norman: University of Oklahoma Press, 1938, rpt. 2002). Richard G. Hardorff provides a treasure trove of primary documents in *Washita Memories: Eyewitness Views of Custer's Attack on Black Kettle's Village* (Norman: University of Oklahoma Press, 2006). Hardorff's footnotes are replete with pertinent information and also well worth reading. His writing style should hold the interest of the sophisticated young scholar. For an account of the 1968 healing ceremony see Raylene Hinz-Penner, "The Washita Site: Finding Sacred Ground" in *Searching for Sacred Ground: The Journey of Chief Lawrence Hart, Mennonite* (Telford, PA: Cascadia Publishing House, 2007), 140–48. For Cheyenne language resources see the *Cheyenne Dictionary* by Louise Fisher, Wayne Leman, Leroy Pine Sr., and Marie Sanchez (Lame Deer, MO: Chief Dull Knife College, 2006).

Names and Terms

To aid the younger scholar and interested reader, a glossary of names and terms is provided.

ame Ame is the Cheyenne word for pemmican, a type of dried meat pounded with native fruit.

Big Hawk Big Hawk is a fictional character. His experiences as a young man striving for manhood, as a hunter, and as Magpie's love interest are based on Cheyenne tribal customs.

Camp Supply Lt. Colonel George Armstrong Custer trekked his men from Camp Supply to Black Kettle's camp. From there he returned to Camp Supply and then to Fort Hays.

Colonel Hazen Colonel William Babcock Hazen, a real person, was no friend to Custer, having testified against him at West Point during Custer's school days. One account (see Brill) speculates that Hazen's testimony helped convict Custer of his first court-martial. It was no secret that Hazen disliked Custer. They did not have the exchange depicted fictionally in this account, although Hazen wrote letters defending Black Kettle's band and tried to protect them.

courtship The courtship of Big Hawk and Magpie is based on Cheyenne courtship patterns. Courtships could take up to five years! In addition to covering his intended with a blanket and talking with her, Big Hawk might have also played Magpie some music on a homemade flute and whispered to her outside her tipi as the family fell asleep. However, one must note that in the strictest Cheyenne sense Big Hawk and Magpie's relationship would likely not be permitted as it is outlined in this story. The taboo against incest reaches beyond our concepts of blood relations. For this reason, in this story Magpie's status as an adopted daughter of Black Kettle and Medicine Woman Later is left deliberately unclear. During this time in Cheyenne history it was not unusual for families to take in orphans. Had Magpie been formally adopted by Black Kettle and Medicine Woman Later, she would have become their daughter and a sister to Big Hawk. A relationship between Big Hawk and Magpie would be considered taboo. In this story, Magpie and Cricket were close to Big Hawk's family but not related. Family status and relationships were complex and made more so by the upheavals of war and the resulting suspended traditions.

Cricket Cricket is a fictional character. In one oral tradition the bones in the Black Kettle Museum were that of a little girl. In a written account, the bones were of a man and were repatriated just before the 1968 reenactment.

Custer George Armstrong Custer's character and responses to the massacre are found in original documents (see Hardorff) and oral traditions. Custer worked closely with General Sheridan, who had control of the land north of the Arkansas River. Sheridan, was determined to exterminate the Cheyennes and all Indians of the Southern Plains south of the Arkansas River. Custer carried out Sheridan's plans. Custer went on to die in the Battle of the Little Bighorn. Some military historians see similar patterns of command between Washita and the Little Bighorn. In both cases, Custer was ill informed and made rash decisions.

Dolores White Calf Dolores White Calf is based on Lucille Young Bull, as found in Mary Jane Warde's account in *Washita*. Her children, Kevin and Nathan, are fictional.

Eonah-pah Eonah-pah, Trailing the Enemy, was a young Kiowa warrior who battled the Seventh Cavalry at Washita. He, along with two Cheyennes, Little Rock (a friend to Black Kettle) and She Wolf, defended about twenty women and children who fled Major Elliott's men and escaped into the Washita River. The three Native Americans set up a defense and saved many lives. During the massacre, Little Rock was killed with a gunshot wound to the head.

family structure Some Cheyennes practiced "sororal polygyny," that is, marriage to sisters. It was not uncommon, especially for chiefs, to take more than one wife. If the man had multiple wives he usually married sisters as it was thought this would limit strife within the family. Sisters raised their offspring together. Everyone's sons and daughters were acknowledged as the offspring of the family grouping. If one mother died, the other mothers continued to raise the children as their own.

Garryowen "Garryowen" is the battle song of the Seventh Cavalry. Custer traveled with a full brass band. Legend has it that it was so cold on the morning of the Washita Massacre that the instruments froze.

giveaways Cheyennes, like many other tribal people, practiced giveaways, large, public giving of gifts to community people and family members. This tradition is still practiced today. Scholars have found that this was a way for Cheyennes to take care of one another and to redistribute the wealth in a tribe—from richer to poorer people.

hardtack Hardtack are army-issue biscuits made of flour, salt, and water, considered to be a flavorless but necessary part of the rank-and-file diet. By contrast, Native Americans, one observer noted, relished eating hardtack, as if eating a wonderful pastry or cake.

haversack These were the sacks issued by the US Army for personal belongings. Soldiers carried haversacks with them as they marched.

heške The Cheyenne word for "mother."

hospitality Cheyenne hospitality traditions required that chiefs and their wives, such as Medicine Woman Later, give food and shelter to all who came seeking it, including enemy scouts and warriors.

ledger art Native American men recorded autobiographical life events such as battles, hunts, and courtship in paint, usually on canvases made of animal hides. After buffalo hides became scarce artists turned to cloth and paper. Ledger paper was common on the plains, hence the name *ledger art*. The ledger art depicted on the front cover of this book depicts women being killed by US Army soldiers.

Luke Walks in the Wind Two Feathers's nephew is fictitious. What is accurate is the relationship between uncle and nephew. In Cheyenne culture, aunts and uncles play important roles in raising the children of their siblings, as do grandparents. It was not unusual for an aunt or uncle to be the primary parent of a niece or nephew.

Magpie There are two persons named Magpie associated with the Washita Massacre. The female, Magpie Woman, was probably in her twenties at the time of the Washita Massacre. Magpie Woman was much older in 1868 than the Magpie in our story. Magpie Woman married George Bent, a well-known interpreter of Cheyenne culture and history. Bent's mother, Owl Woman, was the daughter of an Arrow Keeper, the highest-status chief in Cheyenne society. Bent fought along the Cheyennes at Sand Creek. What little we know of Magpie Woman is because of her famous husband.

Another Magpie experienced the Washita Massacre, the son of Big Man and yet another Magpie Woman. Magpie, an older boy, is thought to be a relative of Black Kettle. Magpie survived the Washita Massacre. He grew up to fight Custer once again, at the Battle of the Little Bighorn. His narrative was collected by Charles J. Brill and is reproduced in Richard G. Hardorff, pp. 301–11 (see above for full citations).

matrilocal bands Cheyennes were matrilocal, meaning that when married the couple lived with the wife's family. They lived in large groups of extended families called bands. Magpie probably lived with her mother's family near her grandmother's tipi.

Medicine Woman Later Medicine Woman Later was one of Black Kettle's wives. She was shot nine times at Sand Creek and survived. She did not survive the Washita Massacre. Cheyenne oral histories and witness accounts document her plea to move the tipis the night before the massacre and her death in the waters of the Washita.

nahaa'e/naxane Cheyennes refer to their father's female relatives, such as aunts and cousins, as *nahaa'e*. Its correct usage is as a familial term. In this story, Magpie uses *nahaa'e* as a term of endearment, much as someone would refer to a favorite older woman as an "aunt." The same is true of *naxane*, which refers to one's paternal male relatives.

place of honor At large community gatherings, Cheyenne chiefs eat last, just as the hunters did at Magpie's camp and like Two Feathers did at the meal following the reenactment. To eat last is a place of honor and also a sign of the chief's caretaker role for his people.

repatriation Repatriation is a process whereby the bones of Native Americans are returned from museums and other holding sites to the tribes. The tribes then bury the bones as befits their traditions and customs.

Ross a.k.a. Bugle Boy Ross is a fictional character. His story was created to depict how some of the rank-and-file members of the Seventh Cavalry experienced the Washita Massacre. Playing "Garryowen," camping in the snow, worrying about supply wagons and frostbite, the killing of the ponies, and the bright star on the morning of the massacre are all found in primary sources.

sacred shawls According to accounts collected by Mary Jane Warde in *Washita*, Lucille Young Bull draped her shawl over the little girl's coffin. Once placed on coffins, shawls become sacred and must, according to Cheyenne tradition, be given away to an honored person.

Sage Woman Sage Woman was one of White Antelope's wives. She died in the Sand Creek Massacre.

sign language Cheyennes, Arapahos, Blackfeet, Kiowas, and Sioux shared a complex and nuanced sign language. Accounts by Spanish-speaking settlers in Texas, US Army personnel on the plains, and Christian missionaries in Indian Territory reference a mellifluous and sophisticated language used between the tribes.

Tsitsistas The Cheyenne tribal name translates to "the People."

travois When Cheyennes moved from the northern woods to the plains they developed a nomadic culture. Initially pulled by dogs and then by horses after their capture, travois carried the band's tipis and household goods as the band traveled from camp to camp.

Two Feathers Two Feathers is based on Cheyenne peace chief Lawrence Hart. The scene in the introduction was real and the author was there. His part of the story is based on a number of conversations and an oral interview with the author and the account of the Washita reenactment found in Raylene Hinz-Penner's book cited above.

ve'ho'e Ve'ho'e is the Cheyenne term for whites. It refers to whites as "spiders" for their technical abilities. It can also mean "trickster." A trickster is a character tribes use as a teaching tool to illustrate what is appropriate behavior. Generally, the trickster disobeys rules and acts in a manner that is not noble.

White Antelope White Antelope was a high-ranking chief and was killed at Sand Creek. He was an ally to Black Kettle, and along with Black Kettle he attempted to secure peace with US Army Major Wynkoop in Denver, Colorado, shortly before the Sand Creek Massacre. White Antelope also went with Black Kettle to Washington, DC, in 1861, where they met with President Lincoln. Lincoln decorated White Antelope with a peace medal.

white flag Though this story positions a lodgepole in the center of camp with the US flag and white flag attached, oral tradition indicates the flags flew from a lodgepole attached to Black Kettle's tipi. Black Kettle erroneously believed his encampment was safe. After all, he raised the US flag given to him by President Lincoln in 1861 along with the white flag symbolizing peace.